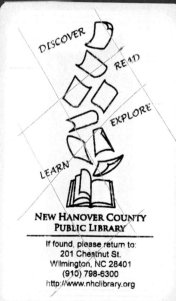

sharks
&
boys

ALSO BY KRISTEN TRACY

A Field Guide for Heartbreakers

sharks & boys

Kristen Tracy

HYPERION
NEW YORK

First Edition

1 3 5 7 9 10 8 6 4 2

V567-9638-5-11105

Printed in the United States of America

Library of Congress Cataloging-in-Publication Data
Tracy, Kristen, 1972–
Sharks & boys / Kristen Tracy.—1st ed.
p. cm.
Summary: Feeling betrayed, fifteen-year-old Enid follows her boyfriend,
Wick, from Vermont to Maryland where he and six others they know
from twin studies rent a yacht, but after she sneaks aboard a storm
sets them adrift without food or water, fighting for survival.
ISBN 978-1-4231-4354-3 (alk. paper)
[1. Survival—Fiction. 2. Interpersonal relations—Fiction.
3. Betrayal—Fiction. 4. Twins—Fiction. 5. Brothers and sisters—Fiction.
6. Ships—Fiction.] I. Title. II. Title: Sharks and boys.
PZ7.T68295Sh 2011
[Fic]—dc22
2011004803

Reinforced binding

Visit www.hyperionteens.com

SUSTAINABLE FORESTRY INITIATIVE   Certified Fiber Sourcing   www.sfiprogram.org

THIS LABEL APPLIES TO TEXT STOCK

For Stephen Colbert—my comedy hero.
Thanks for showing me that laughter is the way.

We had, each of us, a set of wishes.
The number changed. And what we wished—
that changed also. Because
we had, all of us, such different dreams.

from "Fable," Louise Glück

"Enid, it's just a shoe," Wick says.

"I know. But it's my mother's."

"When you tell her the story of what happened to it, I'm sure she won't care that you lost it," Wick says.

"But I'll care."

I don't know why, but my mother's shoe has taken on all this extra meaning. I sit and wait. The shoe bobs merrily along. Eventually, it drifts so close that Landon is able to lean over the side and pluck it from the sea.

"Enjoy," he says, tossing it to me.

I try to slide the shoe on, but my foot is swollen. It hurts. I decide just to hold it.

"Thanks," I say.

"Any time," Landon says. "But I wouldn't expect to come across your other pump. Cherish the one you have."

I press it to my chest and lean back into Wick's arms. I think that I'm going to stay awake and be responsible and totally look for passing ships, but I feel myself dozing off instead.

chapter 1

Three days earlier

Seeing yourself on TV changes you. It just does. Even if you only make the local news. Even if you're part of an unfocused snippet that leads into the afternoon weather update. Three hours ago, when I first saw the story and accompanying footage, I was a butt shot, a footnote, and a blur. I was the sole girl in a line of men on a slow news day in Vermont. Then the segment got rebroadcast relentlessly on all three local networks. I'm in the process of becoming a small-town hero.

"Is that really what my thighs look like?" I ask.

Because Wick and I have been dating for a year, I have asked him questions about my body before, weight-related in particular. He's used to it.

"Your thighs? I can't even see them. You're covered in mud," he says.

"So you're saying I look fat."

I'm standing at the kitchen counter, molding marzipan. We're watching a small television set that my father mounted beneath the cupboard circa 1999. As it turns out, poor pixel quality makes me look comically squat.

"The llama makes you look thinner," he says.

3

I'm rolling the green marzipan into balls now. I have to make eighteen sea urchins for a wedding cake. The bride-to-be has decided to go with a beach theme.

"That llama doesn't look fat," I say. "It looks malnourished."

"That's just because of the mud. It's flattening down its fur," he says. "Can I help? Do you want me to shape the sharks?"

Wick Jarboe is horrible at sculpting marzipan. If I turn the sharks over to him, they'll be indistinguishable from the dolphins.

"How about you make the shoes?"

Wick shoves his hands in his pockets.

"The shoes are for the bride and groom. They're what sit directly on the cake. They're, like, almost the most important part of the whole thing."

He pulls his hands out of his pockets, and I think he's going to reach toward me or the marzipan, but he doesn't. His skin is rough and tanned. He's been biking a lot this summer, so his arms and the majority of his legs have turned an attractive bronze shade. My skin will never turn that color. I'm a burner. When I stop staring at Wick's arms and glance at his face, I notice that he isn't even watching the llama news clip anymore. He's looking out the window.

"What do you see?" I ask.

Sometimes my neighbor, an elementary-school teacher still in her twenties, likes to garden in her bikini. Wick turns his attention to me again. He's standing in a shaft of sun, making his brown hair appear almost golden.

"What sort of shoes should the groom wear?" Wick asks.

"Black tuxedo shoes," I say.

Wick joins me and tears a piece of black marzipan from a large ball. I watch his long, lean arms drape over my kitchen table, blue veins branching at his wrists. He's wearing a green rubber bracelet. It's meant to raise awareness for nonspecific environmental issues. We bought a pair of them together at a shop on Church Street. But I lost my original months ago. I have small hands. It must have just slipped off and fallen into the gutter or something. The one I'm wearing now, my replacement bracelet, is a slightly brighter shade than Wick's.

"You'd think a person wouldn't want to wear a bikini and groom her magnolia tree at the same time."

I stop sculpting sea urchins and frown at him. "So you were watching her?"

He shrugs. "It was a glance."

It does not comfort me to think that my boyfriend is a *glancer*. I exhale loudly and resume sculpting. Wick gets back to work too. He may be a thin guy, but his thumbs are thick. He's able to mold the shoes into oblong chunks, but they don't quite resemble tuxedo shoes.

"What is the bride wearing?" he asks.

"You choose. Make them white. And nothing strippery."

"Strippery?"

"No stripper footwear." I make sure to keep my voice

light and playful so he knows I'm kidding around.

Wick winks at me, then reaches for a gob of white marzipan. He takes a much smaller amount than he did of the black. I guess he assumes that all brides' feet are Cinderella-like and dainty.

"*Stay tuned to watch the amazing story of a local llama rescue*," a reporter says.

I watch Wick's face. He looks bored.

"Aren't you impressed at all that I jumped in that mud hole with a bunch of construction workers?" I ask.

"Yeah," he says.

But I want more. It's like I need more assurance than Wick is equipped to give me. It's as if in recent weeks all the insecure feelings inside of me have grown too big for my body. I feel like I could break open.

"I saw an animal in trouble, and I didn't even hesitate," I say.

"Are you calling me out?" he asks. Wick drops the marzipan shoes. "You know, somebody had to call the proper authorities for help."

This is terrible. He thinks I am criticizing either his judgment or his masculinity. But I wasn't trying to do that. I just wanted him to reaffirm my own bravery. Again. "I'm not calling you out. You were awesome. You told the neighbor to dial 9-1-1."

"We were in a very remote area. I didn't realize that one of the construction workers had cell phone reception. I had no idea the fire department was already on its way."

"I know. I know," I say. I reach across the table and

gently take hold of his arm. "You're missing my point. I'm saying that I saw an animal in trouble, and I recognized that there were two sides. Side death or side llama—and I chose side llama, and I stayed committed to that side."

"I think we were all on side llama," Wick says.

He's worked the bride's shoes into long strings. They're almost formless. They look like noodles. I consider saying something, but then I notice that his fingers are sweating. This is awful. For sanitation reasons, he's going to have to start over.

"You can't sweat on the marzipan," I say. "People are going to eat it."

Wick rolls his eyes. "Nobody eats the bride and groom."

"When they're made out of plastic, you're right. But these are made specifically to be eaten."

"Did the bride request an edible version of herself? That's wrong on so many levels. I mean, who's going to eat her?"

"I think the groom," I say.

Wick flicks one of the shoe-noodles with his finger and sends it rolling across the table.

"Are we still talking about marzipan?" he asks with a tone of mock boredom.

"Yeah. Do you want to talk about something else?"

I've finished shaping the sea urchins. It's time to add some vibrancy. By hand-brushing the candy with varying shades of powdered green food coloring, and leaving five pairs of white bands, I'm making the round shells look incredibly lifelike. Wick flicks the other shoe-noodle. This one sails across the counter and sticks to the television screen. They're showing it again. A group of five construction workers and I are pulling an exhausted llama from a mud hole. The llama's owner videotaped it. Wick leans over and turns off the television.

I dip the brush in the dark green powder and press the color into the round top of the ball. My mother assures me that it's these small details that have given her such a bang-up reputation as a decorator.

"I wonder if this will become a national story? Who doesn't want to see a llama escape the maw of a deadly mud hole?" I say.

"The maw?" he asks. He's peeling the marzipan from the TV screen with his fingernail.

"It means mouth," I say.

"I know. I played the tuba," he says. "It's what my teacher called the bell."

It seems odd to be bringing this up, because Wick hasn't touched a tuba since junior high.

"How many times do I need to congratulate you about the rescue? Please, Enid, just give me a number."

Wick stands up. I don't.

"A boyfriend is supposed to be a support system," I say. "Not part of the time, but all of the time. And you, well, you're so sporadic."

"You're calling me sporadic?" He points to himself and releases a noise I've never heard before. It's a cross between a sound of surrender and a sound of disgust.

I point at him too and repeat, "Sporadic."

"Is this about the e-zine?" Wick asks. "It's been three months. Are you still hung up on that?" He folds his arms across his chest.

I'm not too surprised that we're here again. We haven't had a fight over the e-zine catastrophe in over a week.

"I didn't have anything to do with it," he says.

Now I stand. Sitting feels too passive. "Your brother drew the cartoons!" I say. I don't know who came up with the initial idea to write, illustrate, and circulate a group of poorly rhymed sonnets that mocked several high school girls during exam week. But I do know who executed the idea: Burr Riggs and his brother, Skate. And Dale Jarboe.

"But I didn't make the e-zine!" Wick says. He throws his hands up in the air, making his defense look more dramatic.

"You knew they were up to something," I say. "Burr and Skate have been acting like maniacs. And your brother is hardwired to be a terrible and inappropriate person ninety-four percent of the time."

"It *was* terrible. They shouldn't have done it. But you need to get to a place of forgiveness about this. Skate and Burr are grieving. Their parents just died. They exercised poor judgment. You're being way too hard on them," Wick says.

Even if Wick is right, I am still so humiliated by the sonnet that was written about me, and the demoralizing cartoon depiction that was drawn beside it rendering me with a pig nose, hairy chest, and no neck, to get beyond it. At one point, I was friends with all of them except for Dale. I can't believe I was one of their e-zine targets.

Wick's face is pink, and he's running his fingers through his hair. I'm not sure how he got so upset. I'm the one who's earned the right to be upset. Can he not see that? It must be a guy thing. I don't get the male mind. I have a twin brother, and it's still a complete enigma.

"What they did was vulgar," I say.

"When you get upset about something, you're like a dog with a bone," Wick says.

"So now you're calling me a dog," I say. "Great."

"You know I'm not calling you a dog."

He's right. I know that. I see him glance out the window again, and I cringe.

"Can you lay off ogling my neighbor while we fight?" I say.

"Why are you so angry at me?" he asks.

He raises a good question. But I don't think that I'm *that* angry with him.

I reach for his hand, but he pulls away.

"Let's not argue anymore," I say. I'm sick of the tension. I want to be getting along again.

"I need to tell you something," he says.

These are not the words a girl wants to hear her boyfriend say during a fight.

"What?" I reach out to take his hand again. This time he lets me.

"I want to go to the party," he says.

I hear myself gasp.

"Skate and Burr's parents were killed six months ago, Enid. They've been acting a little crazy, but I'm not going to write them off. I'm not a jerk."

Is the implication here that *I'm* a jerk?

I shake my head. Doesn't Wick understand that this feels like a betrayal? The final quatrain of the sonnet titled "Enid Walking Home" flashes through my mind.

Enid stomps home like a boot-skirt sage
Her tight butt clenched in a fit of rage.
Never tell Enid she's wrong not right
Her cheeks might rupture, for they are that tight.

I repeat the last quatrain for Wick.

"They didn't mean it. It doesn't even make sense. Seriously, Enid. It's nonsense."

As he talks he backs up a little and turns his body. His sneakers are aimed away from me.

"You can't go," I say. Burr and Skate have been planning their postgraduation party for months, even before the accident. I heard Burr talking about it in biology. It's at their uncle's house in Maryland. "There's no need to commute that far for a party unless you have very devious plans."

"I can't go? Enid, it's not like we're married," he says, pointing to the marzipan.

"It's not like you're single," I say, pointing to myself.

Wick is so frustrated that he squeezes his lips together, erasing their pinkness, turning them white. "High school is supposed to be about having fun," he says.

"Well, if that's true, pretty much the entire educational system needs to be overhauled."

"Enid, we've been dating for a year."

I feel a pain beneath my breastbone. I have been in love with Wick Jarboe since the moment I saw him. I was six. He was seven. He was holding an iguana. I thought it was a dinosaur. He wanted me to pet it. But I ran off screaming instead. Love.

"You're thinking about the iguana, aren't you?" he asks.

"No," I say. I guess I've brought up the iguana more than I realized. "I just don't know where you're going with this."

"Your brother's coming," he says.

"What?" I don't believe this.

"Sov and Munny will be there too," he says. "And Dale."

With my palm, I smash a sea urchin flat as a pancake. I can't believe the Paddingtons are letting their sons go.

"Skate and Burr and your obnoxious brother should not be corrupting Sov and Munny. They're, like, the most innocent Cambodian twins I've ever met."

"They're probably the only Cambodian twins you'll ever meet. And they're half Irish. So they're only half Cambodian."

I shrug. I don't feel like being corrected or talking about Sov and Munny.

"Guys are guys. We need to blow off some steam."

"Is Simone going to be there?" I ask.

We live in Vermont. The party is in Maryland. Simone, a perpetual flirt from the swim team, moved to Virginia at the beginning of the year. She was always interested in Wick and was always trying to catch his eye during practice. She was the sort of girl who seemed to be bending over right when a guy arrived. There's a possibility that she could be going. Geographically speaking, it's very doable.

"Simone isn't coming. I barely know her. It's just guys."

I don't believe him.

I imagine Wick making out with Simone. I imagine Wick getting drunk with Simone. I imagine Wick impregnating Simone. I imagine myself married to Wick and raising Simone's difficult and moody love child. I have always hated Simone.

"I feel like I'm stuck in a net," he says. He lets go of my hand and throws his arms out in front of himself, like he's struggling to swim through the air. "A relationship shouldn't feel this way. It should be fun."

"Like high school," I offer, turning my body away.

His arms fall to his sides.

"We're too serious. We're making marzipan together in your mother's kitchen on a Friday afternoon. And it's still summer."

He says it like he's disgusted with himself. The pain beneath my breastbone deepens.

"Don't you like hanging out with me?" I ask.

"It's not you, Enid," he says. "It's me."

And now I feel trapped too. Like I've been flung into one of those horrible after-school specials.

"Do you know what I did yesterday?" he asks.

I'm afraid to guess.

"I donated a hundred dollars to Greenpeace to help save the menhaden off the coast of Maryland."

"That's great," I say.

Menhaden are fish. Wick found out about their over-fished and dwindling population near the Chesapeake Bay. At high school, we're seen as an environmentalist couple. I'm more concerned about saving whales and elephants and cool-looking tigers and stuff. But I totally support his menhaden position.

Wick groans, walks toward me, then places his hand over the groom's shoes and squishes them. It's sort of a relief to see this. I mean, I wasn't going to be able to use those.

"What's so bad about giving money to Greenpeace?" I ask.

"Enid, I'm way too responsible. I shouldn't be worried about environmental issues until I'm in my thirties."

He tugs at his green rubber bracelet until it slides off his wrist. None of this makes any sense. I don't know what to do. Should I offer to go do something reckless with him to make him feel better?

"Don't," I say.

He pauses, slides the bracelet back on his wrist, and I'm relieved. Maybe I can fix this.

"I think we need a break," he says.

I bite my lip. Maybe I can't fix this. It feels like an ax has fallen. A sharp pain radiates through me, and every time I blink, when I reopen my eyes, the world looks a little darker.

"I think we should talk more," I say. I want him to change his mind.

"After the party," he says.

"You can't go to the party."

I can feel him slipping away, and I don't want to let him go. Not to the party. Not ever.

"A break makes sense," he says.

Just an hour ago, I felt so good. Now the ache beneath my breastbone is so strong that I lift my hand and rub my chest.

"We'll talk more next week," he says. "I'll call you."

I don't say anything. I watch him walk out of my house. I hear him start his car. I hear his tires turn gravel over in my driveway. A part of me cannot believe this is happening. But another part of me knows that I've just been dumped.

chapter 2

My mother is inspecting my killer whales. She turns one upside down and runs her fingertip over its belly. Then she sets it with the rest of the herd. Or pod. Or whatever you call a group of marzipan killer whales on their way to a wedding where they will be eaten by half-drunk guests.

"You do such a great job with the tails," she says. "The fluting is impeccable."

My mother kisses my head. She's already approved of my lobsters, crabs, dolphins, sharks, sea urchins, starfish, and sperm whales. Now it's time to show her the bride and groom. I don't have a steady enough hand to paint on the faces. She does that. I surrender two slim figures absent their eyes, noses, and mouths.

"Great shoes," she says. "But aren't the bride's a little small?"

I nod. In a moment of nostalgia, I decided to overlook the sanitation risk and mold the bride's pumps and the groom's tuxedo shoes out of what remained of Wick's failed attempts. It's not like sweat can kill you. At least, probably not Wick Jarboe's sweat. Following their assembly, I dusted the shoes with edible glitter. They shimmer and look spectacular.

My mother picks up a paint brush to add the final

details. But her hand shakes. She sets down the brush and rubs her eyes.

"I'm tired," she says.

I'm not surprised to hear this. She and my father attend couples therapy on Friday afternoons. She never arrives home from her session in stellar condition. It must be difficult to face all that truth, to hear about the other women. I hate to admit this, but my father is such a cad.

"The reception is at three. We set up at eleven. I can draw the faces in the morning."

I nod again.

"Are you okay?" she asks.

I nod, but then stop midway through. Why lie to my mother?

"Today sort of sucked for me."

"Was it a twin day?" she asks.

I shake my head no. My mother overestimates the demands placed on me when I go to twin studies. She thinks that because I'm the only girl, they're somehow more difficult for me. But that's not true. Twin studies are easy. I like them. Once a month, Landon and I join three sets of identical twins for a series of tests: Sov and Munny, Wick and Dale, and Skate and Burr. All the data they gather is supposedly meant to measure our twinergy levels. Except, they're scientists, and they don't call it that.

"Twin Friday is next week," I say. "Today sucked for other reasons."

"Tell me what's wrong."

I don't know where to start. My father is living in the

basement. The distance between me and Wick feels as big as Antarctica. And the pain beneath my breastbone is still there. But she's so fresh back from her counseling session that I'm afraid if I try to talk about relationship issues, she'll try to speak to me in therapy language. I hate that.

"I don't know," I say.

I want to tell her about the llama drama, but I don't. Hypothetically, yesterday and today were supposed to be dedicated solely to molding marzipan. Due to the complicated nature of the beach theme, she was concerned that I wouldn't be able to finish. At least not to her standards.

"Biting into our marzipan shouldn't be an easy act," she had said this morning on her way out the door. "There needs to be a moment of hesitation. I want them to wrestle with what they're about to do."

"Okay," I said. "But shouldn't we want the guest to enjoy eating what we've made, instead of feeling racked with guilt for biting into a sugar-based starfish?"

"I want them to fully appreciate what we've made before they let their teeth and spit dismantle it."

Why my mother feels the need to develop a code of ethics for marzipan consumption is complicated, creepy, and most likely related to my adulterating father.

She envelops the bride and groom in plastic wrap.

"Is your brother home?" she asks.

I shake my head no.

The last I saw of Landon he was headed out to go biking around Lake Champlain. As he walked through the door in his tight biker shorts and neon-striped shirt, I considered asking him if he was biking alone or meeting up with somebody. But I didn't. I might have been afraid of the answer. Before the e-zine, Landon and I often biked around on Fridays with Skate and Burr. After my falling out with them, the biking ceased. But for the last couple of weeks, Landon has picked it up again.

"Did he go biking?" my mother asks.

I nod.

"With Skate and Burr?"

I shrug. Then frown. Then shrug again. "Probably."

"You're giving that stupid sonnet way too much power."

"Maybe," I half admit.

"If you stay hung up on that, it's going to start affecting your relationship with Wick."

My mother is a mind reader. Which is probably how she was able to figure out my father's latest affair. I look at the ceiling. I look at her. Why not just tell her?

"It already has affected it. We're taking a break."

My mother walks toward me and gives me a prolonged hug. "No wonder your day sucked. That's terrible news."

"It's not terrible. We're not totally broken up. It's a break. People take them all the time."

"Be careful, Enid. Think of the larger group here. You don't want to ostracize yourself over this situation."

This is something my mother should have told me three months ago when I did not consider the larger group and began to ostracize myself over this situation.

She releases her hug and continues to rub my back.

"Do you want to know what I think is going on?" she asks.

I'm too tired to be psychoanalyzed.

"It's your way of grieving."

I really don't want to be having this conversation. I know it was an unspeakable accident. It was a tragedy. And of course I am still grieving for Mr. and Mrs. Riggs. And for Skate and Burr too. But a tragedy doesn't give somebody license to do anything they want. You still have to be a responsible human being. You have to keep being nice.

"You're pulling away to protect yourself. You're angrier than you need to be, because it's your way of keeping distance from Burr and Skate. Because deep down, they are your friends. They're like our own family, Enid."

I feel myself holding back tears. "I don't want to talk about this anymore."

Maybe my mother is right, but at the moment I don't want to think about it. I actually try not to think about Mr. and Mrs. Riggs very much at all. Because thinking about them won't bring anybody back. It just makes me sad. We used to barbecue with them almost every Sunday during the summer. Mr. Riggs grilled the meat. A few times we traveled to Maine together to camp in Acadia. Their absence is something that I purposely ignore.

"They're good kids. It's going to take them time," my mother says. "But they'll get there."

She is a much more sympathetic person than I am. And this realization makes me feel rotten.

"I guess," I say. Even during the good times Skate and Burr were hopelessly immature. They wore stupid T-shirts with juvenile messages printed across their chests. Burr's: I'VE UPPED MY STANDARDS, SO UP YOURS. And Skate's: I CAN'T, I'M MORMON. Skate and Burr talk about being Mormon quite a bit. But they don't behave like they come from a conservative religious persuasion. Presbyterians, maybe.

As my mother and I place the marzipan pieces in Tupperware containers, I'm tempted to tell her about the llama adventure. I want her to see how strong and brave I was. But I was supposed to be home wrestling almond paste into sea creatures. Not off fooling around with Wick. I mean, we weren't really fooling around in a sexual sense. Frankly, the llama catastrophe came upon us before we even got to consider that.

My mother presses the lid closed on the last container. "Great job. Thanks for sacrificing your Friday. Maybe next week will suck less."

If I had the words to explain my feelings, I would give them to her. But I don't.

"I can only hope," I say.

"Enid, things will get better." Even though she delivers this statement with complete certainty, it feels like a guess.

"I want to share something I learned today in therapy," she says.

I have no desire to hear about the intimate details of my father's betrayal. I wrinkle my face. "Please, nothing graphic."

"Sit down." My mother pulls out a chair and I pull out a chair, and we sit across the table from each other with a wall of Tupperware between us. "You're one of the main reasons I go to therapy."

This surprises me because I consider myself a fairly easy-to-raise daughter.

"I want you to seek out a healthy dynamic with a man. I don't want you to accept your father's behavior as normal."

"I don't," I say. "I know he's a pig."

To say that the relationship I have with my father is complicated is an understatement. Up until counseling started, he often spoke about the need to fulfill the thrill. Presumably this statement referred to everything from skydiving, which he's done numerous times, to boinking his secretary, which he's also done numerous times.

"People aren't perfect. If you focus solely on the ways they've disappointed you, you'll wind up a perpetually wounded person."

I shrug again. "You're being way too easy on him." I think of Wick. I think of Simone. I think of my bikini-clad neighbor. Some naïve person centuries ago said that love is blind. I wish that were true. I wish that once you fell in love with a person that you both went blind to everyone else, especially attractive people. Life would be much simpler.

My mother doesn't say anything as she stands. She walks down the hallway toward her bedroom and says, "Don't stay angry. It will eat you up." She closes the door.

I don't think I'm that angry. I pop off one of the Tupper-ware lids so I can look at my sea urchins one last time. Staring at them lined up into four tidy rows gives me a real sense of accomplishment. I replace the lid and walk to my room. My father isn't home yet from couples ther-apy. He has a separate session after their dual session. The therapy started three months ago. My mother thinks it began twenty years too late.

chapter 3

Sleep did not come easy last night. The pain beneath my breastbone spread. I just lay there on my bed and physically ached. It's like I'd been hit by a Mack truck hauling two tons of heartache. I want to call Wick. But I'm not an idiot. I know that such a move on my part would probably push him further away. It's exactly like Pam Van Dorn used to say: "A relationship is like a rubber band."

The first time I heard about the rubber-band principle was in eighth grade during lunch. Pam and I were sitting together on the front lawn, sharing her ham sandwich. She held a rubber band between her two index fingers.

"Tension is good. It's what you want. But when I start doing this"—she moved one of her index fingers closer to the other one—"I lose the tension. And the relationship ends."

I watched the rubber band slide down her finger and dangle in the air.

"So I'm a finger?" I asked her. "And the guy I like is the other finger?"

"Exactly," she said. "And the relationship is the rubber band. And that's why you should never chase a guy. When you move closer, you lose the tension, ultimately dooming your relationship to be nothing more than a flaccid loop of elastic."

I stared at the dangling loop.

"Okay," I said. "But using this model, you never get to touch your guy." I held my fingers up and imagined a rubber band stretching between them and two people never meeting. Love seemed hopeless.

Pam took a big bite of her sandwich and shook her head. "The rubber band is a psychological metaphor. Physical stuff works differently. You're totally allowed to touch your guy."

"Cool," I said.

Pam was always so smart about life. And she had an impressive vocabulary. Plus, her mom made pretty good ham sandwiches. We were close all through junior high. Then she started dating Billy Rome and I started dating Wick, and my life took off in a new direction.

In hindsight, our coupling seemed destined. The year before we dated, Wick and I had the same biology class. We knew each other, obviously, from twin studies. And we were both on the swim team. And we'd had that early iguana encounter. But even though fate had put us in the same classroom five days a week, and in the same swimming pool twice a week, nearly the whole year passed before something romantic happened.

Then, there was the field survey assignment during summer break. There were a dozen different things you could do. Test water at Lake Champlain. Sample soil in Waterbury near the Ben & Jerry's ice cream factory.

Collect and dissect flowers near the Trapp Family Lodge in Stowe. Wick and I ended up in the same field survey. We both signed up to take granite samples from Rock of Ages in Barre. I don't even care about granite. I don't even know how it happened. One day, I drove to Barre to complete a boring assignment. The next thing I knew I spotted Wick's head a few people in front of me in line at the granite quarry.

He was so mature. He saw me and made his way to me. And so we toured the whole quarry together. Laughing at each other's mausoleum jokes. Offering each other breath mints and pieces of chewing gum. And then, afterward, instead of getting into our separate cars and driving back to Burlington, he suggested getting a panini at a restaurant in Montpelier. And he didn't stop dialing up the romance there. When we got to Sarducci's, instead of letting us take a table indoors, he requested a table on the patio that overlooked the Winooski River.

He was a prince. He didn't sit there and talk about himself while he ate his sandwich. He asked me a lot of questions about my life. He wanted to hear my thoughts on everything from deforestation to the flat tax. We talked about Pablo Neruda's poetry and Nadine Gordimer's short stories. He asked me personal questions about what it felt like to be a fraternal twin. I mean, he was curious about how I perceived my individual identity. It reminded me of the phrase "fit like a hand in a glove." During our panini moment, Wick was the hand and I was the glove.

And when I thought things couldn't get any better,

the most mind-blowing thing happened: everything got better. Wick started talking about how we seemed to be in each other's orbits: biology, swim class, twin studies. And I loved that idea. I wanted to think of myself as a moon or maybe a planet being drawn to another moon. Like the path I was on with Wick was more significant than anything on earth; it was celestial.

And then, right when the check came and he paid for my panini, Wick said things that were so mature it made me question whether I was mature enough to be in Wick's orbit. He said, "I've liked you for a while. We should do more stuff together." And that's when I realized that the granite quarry hadn't been a coincidence. Because Wick said, "I asked Mr. Tober which field study you were doing."

After that our orbits merged, and we began going out for sushi, and turnovers, and foreign films. Pam used to say that falling in love is all about meeting the right person in the right circumstance. God, she was smart. Maybe I should call her and solicit some advice. She and Billy are still going strong. She must know something about interpreting male behavior that I don't. I try to stop myself from thinking about Wick and guys. I force myself to get out of bed. I must get up.

After contemplating getting dressed but deciding not to, I walk toward the kitchen. I should make some toast. Or pour a glass of orange juice. But I'm not hungry. I feel broken and empty in a way that doesn't require food. When I reach the end of the hallway, it's as if the kitchen phone wants to jump out of its cradle and leap into my hands. I pause at the doorjamb. If I called Wick right now, what would I say?

"*Wick, I think the universe has a plan for us.*"

"*Wick, come over and I'll let you eat marzipan off my body.*"

"*Wick, one day I hope to have your babies. And you're tall and I'm short and that's going to hurt.*"

It's such a good thing that Pam told me about the rubber-band principle. This breakup is hitting me like a wave. Two minutes ago I was reasonably okay. But now I'm not. *Do not call Wick. Take a deep breath. Seek out some male perspective.*

"Enid, get out of my room."

Landon can be so annoying. As my brother, as my twin, he should *want* to talk to me. Even if it is six o'clock in the morning.

"I didn't sleep well," I say.

"I was doing fine until a few minutes ago."

"I've got a lot on my mind."

Landon pulls his comforter over his head and rolls onto his stomach. He leaves a shoulder uncovered, and I can see underarm hair sprouting out of his pit.

"Have you talked to Wick? Did he tell you what happened?"

He doesn't answer. I always assume that silence means yes.

"I don't think it's a permanent break. He said we'd talk next week. But I'm a little worried about this party."

I sit at the foot of his bed.

28

"Don't you have any advice?" I ask. "By the way, I'm crying."

Landon rolls onto his back and pushes his comforter down so he can see my face.

"Don't cry," he says.

I wasn't crying, but I frown dramatically so he thinks I'm more despondent than desperate. I want him to tell me everything he knows.

"So you think it's not permanent either?" I ask.

He props himself up on his elbows. His hair is lying on top of his head in a flat brown mess. Somehow sleep has unwound his curls.

"I have no idea what's going on with Wick."

"So he hasn't mentioned any other girls?"

Landon doesn't say anything.

"Has he been talking about Simone? Because that would be so stupid. She lives hundreds of miles away. Maybe she'd be good for a fling or something. But with the price of gas these days, there's no way that she's girl-friend material, right?"

Landon falls back onto his bed.

"It's too early for this," he says.

"So you think he'll have a fling?" I ask.

"You sound like Mom," he says.

I bite my lip and suck on it. I'm pretty much a normal teenager, and I don't want to sound like my mother. Especially since mine is in the throes of a deeply dysfunctional relationship that even counseling doesn't seem capable of setting right.

"Who uses the word 'fling' anymore? You're asking me if Wick would hook up with a hot girl who has long-standing interest in him? I guess it's possible."

To my surprise, now I really am crying.

"Don't say that." I let the tears run down my face.

"I'm just being honest," he says.

"But if he did do that, if he hooks up with Simone, maybe he and I could still work things out, right?"

"Is that what you'd want?"

"I love him," I say. "I really do."

Landon sits up. He blinks at me. "Enid, you're too young to love a guy." He grabs a tissue from a box beside his bed and hands it to me. "It hurts now, but you'll move through it. It's part of life."

"Or we could get back together," I say.

"You're thinking like a girl, Enid."

"I am a girl."

"Try to think like a guy."

I shake my head. "But I'm not attracted to Simone."

Landon scratches his head and yawns.

"Listen, the thing about guys is, well, we're animals. You want us to be all kind and cuddly, like baby ducks or something. But we're not. We're visual beasts."

"So you're saying Simone looks better than I do?"

"You're thinking like a girl again. I can safely speak for all straight guys when I say that when it comes to the female population, we really like to look, and we're always tempted to pursue."

"You're not helping me at all," I say.

Landon unleashes another yawn. I feel like I'm boring him. And that hurts too.

"Enid, you need to give him space. Dudes love space."

"But if I give him too much space, he'll leave my orbit."

"Your orbit? You can't control what happens. If Wick moves on, Wick moves on. And you'll meet somebody else. You're a great catch, Enid. You're nice. You bake cakes. You're smart. You swim."

Landon has no clue what a brokenhearted girl wants to hear. I ignore much of what he just said and roll down onto my side. "But it hasn't even been a whole day yet. Has he told you he's moving on?"

He shakes his head no. "I'm just thinking like a guy."

"He can't."

"He's a guy. He's going to move on."

"God, Landon, you make it sound like you're all apex predators. You're wrong about a lot of things. First, I don't bake cakes; I decorate them. Second, Wick is not moving on. Third, I saved a llama yesterday and that makes me more than a good catch; it makes me brave and totally interesting."

He lies back down.

"Enid, I don't want to argue with you. I accept point one. And I caution you against deluding yourself by believing point two. And I saw point three on the news last night. That's too bad."

"What do you mean that's too bad? What do you have against llamas?"

"It died."

31

"No, that's not the story. It almost died and then I helped save it."

"After that, it died. I saw it late last night on the news."

"Are you serious?"

"As a heart attack," he says. He buries his head under his pillow. "Go online and see for yourself."

I hurry to his computer desk and open up his laptop.

"Can't you check it out in your room?" he asks.

I ignore him. I Google: llama rescue in Burlington, Vermont. The stories pop up. I click onto the first link. He wasn't lying. The llama did die.

"Its name was Pilsner Urquell," I say. "His owner said he was twenty-two and died of natural causes. Or possibly exhaustion."

"Twenty-two is a lot of years for a llama."

I didn't save anything. I'm not a hero. Nothing about me is special. I'm a nice high school junior who decorates cakes and swims. This makes me freaking dull.

I close his laptop and get ready to leave. I've got an entire lame day ahead of me. I have marzipan to arrange and a wedding cake to assemble. I pat Landon's computer. It didn't mean to deliver soul-crushing news.

"Are you hitting my laptop?" Landon asks.

"No."

And it's at this moment that I see the symbol of my relationship with Wick lying on Landon's desk like a sign. It's a rubber band. I pick it up. I place my index fingers inside it and stretch it out. I make it taut. I hold it that way and stare into it like I'm looking at my own heart. I mimic Wick's flight and pull one of my fingers away from the other. And then it happens. The band snaps. It sails away. My hand stings so badly that I rub it against my pajama bottoms. I reach to pick the elastic up. But I can't find it. Oh my God. There's a message in this. Too much tension can break the band, thus resulting in a broken piece of rubber that can totally zoom out of your life and disappear.

I'm about to get on my knees and try to recover my tragic symbol, when I notice something else. It's a second sign, nestled in a wire basket sitting on top of Landon's desk. It's directions to the party. I touch the paper and trace my finger south along I-87. All of a sudden, this amazing energy crawls up my hand and arm. This must be how people who get struck by lightning feel. (Minus the singed hair, scorched clothing, and burned flesh.)

I feel as though I've been led to these papers by a higher source. It's like the story of Moses being found in the bulrushes, or swamp, or wherever. Just like the woman who was guided to find the baby in the basket and save his life, I've been led to find these pieces of paper in this basket and save my relationship with Wick. I feel a deep gratitude for both MapQuest and the Bible classes my grandmother took me to as a child.

As I lift the pages out of the basket, I look back at Landon. His comforter rises and falls. He's sleeping. He won't know that I've taken them. Careful to avoid making any noise, I slowly fold the papers into a square and stick them inside my back pocket. With my breath held, I back out of Landon's doorway, and cautiously close the door as I go.

Walking past the kitchen, I unfortunately see my father. He's at the table by himself, drinking coffee. I quicken my pace. Currently, I'm avoiding him. This is due to reasons that I have yet to disclose to anyone, because they reflect poorly on me as a human being. I guess it's safe to say that my father is not the only one living down a mistake.

"Enid?" he says.

I basically run to the bathroom and lock the door. I hear him walking down the hallway. I turn the shower on full blast. He knocks. His thuds sound urgent.

"We're going to have to talk about this sooner or later," he says.

Um, if that's a choice, I select later. He knocks again. Even his knocking sounds disappointed with me. And that's not fair. Because what right does he have to be disappointed with me? He's the one who set everything in motion. He made the storm. All I'm trying to do now is weather the sea. Given all the drama he's introduced to my life, I'm bound to make a few mistakes. I close the toilet and sit on the lid.

"There's better ways to handle this," he says. "Calling her and saying those things doesn't solve anything. This isn't her fault."

He didn't need to tell me that. I know the phone call wasn't a solution. There is no solution to this problem. Plus, I'm one of those people who's always in touch with her failings. I pick up a shampoo bottle and try to read the ingredients. It's not much of a distraction, but I need something. First I lose Wick. Then the llama dies. And now my father is trying to force a confrontation with me about a situation that I have no desire to discuss. I toss the shampoo bottle into the tub. Then I press down on the handle and flush the toilet.

"I'm late for work. Honey, we'll talk tonight," he says.

I don't say anything. I mean, whatever. Who works on a Saturday? And why is he calling me honey? He hasn't earned that. Don't you have to forgive somebody before they can start referring to you by pet names? Isn't this a rule that's well documented in etiquette columns across nearly all civilizations? I hear the front door slam shut. Rather than turn off the shower, I decide to take one.

Naked and lonely, I step into the warm flood of water. As much as I want to, I don't think I can abandon my mother and run off to Maryland to stop this stupid party. The reasons are infinite. I don't have a car. I'm somewhat of a coward. The wedding is big. I'm responsible. I love my mother, and the event isn't something she can handle alone. And how does one go about stopping a party anyway?

chapter 4

"Lift with your knees," my mother says.

"Don't you mean your legs? How do you lift with your knees?" I ask.

Gary, one of the groomsmen, has offered to help us haul in all five tiers of the cake. My mother is instructing him on the proper way to carry it. I feel itchy. Eager to improve my mood, my mother suggested that I wear a skirt while we were getting ready this morning. Normally I wear black pants to help her set up for receptions. The skirt is like nothing I would ever wear; it's white. And embossed with a countless number of fleurs-de-lis. I look like a fancy handkerchief. I miss my pants, which I surrendered way too easily on the heels of the following conversation:

Her: "Why not dress up? Weddings are great places to meet people."

Me: "By people do you mean men?"

Her: "I've got a skirt that will fit you perfectly and really show off your slim waist."

Me: "For work, I find skirts limiting. We're going to be setting up. There'll be a ton of lifting and bending."

Her: "It's not like factory labor. And a new man is a great way to get over the last man."

Me: "Give me the skirt."

Her: "I've got classy heels to go with it."

Me: "Are they white?"

Her: "What else would you wear with a white skirt?"

Me: "I'm going to feel like a nurse."

Her: "But with the right blouse, you sure won't look like one."

Which is how I ended up in this itchy, man-catching getup. That's one of the strange things about my mother. Because she's saddled to a bad one, she resents men, yet she deeply believes that every woman needs one to be complete. I think my mother might actually be a misogynist.

I watch Gary steady the lowest and biggest tier of the cake on the bumper of my mother's new Subaru. The frosting is so close to the ridge of the trunk that it will almost inevitably get smeared and need a touch-up. I look at my mother. She isn't breathing. I look back to Gary. He has a goatee and is an awkward guy, not the kind of person you can totally trust with a wedding cake. Had we been characters in a situation comedy, Gary would have already stumbled over his patent leather shoes and planted his face in the cake's perfect center.

"Have you got it?" my mother asks.

"All set," he says.

He hefts it up over his head like a waiter lifts a tray, and walks into the reception hall.

"Gary is going to give me a stroke," my mother says.

"I'll take the fourth tier. You take the third. We'll beat him back here and take the second and first ourselves," I say. "That way we take Gary out of the picture."

My mother smiles. "Good."

Usually I like carrying cake. It smells good and requires your full attention. The cake is at your mercy. You've got to stay balanced and focused and aware of its delicately iced boundaries. But carrying cake today makes me feel like a drag. I'm boring. Even Gary doesn't seem interested in me. And I look incredible today; he should totally be interested in me. But he's not. Also, it's no fun carrying cake while wearing uncomfortable heels.

After dropping off our tiers, my mother and I manage to beat Gary back to the car.

"I bet there are guys more suited for you inside," my mom says.

I roll my eyes. "I don't *need* a guy."

"You know what I mean."

"Isn't the ratio in Canada better? If I ever get desperate, shouldn't I hightail it north?" I ask.

We hear a shuffling sound, and both jump, fearing Gary's return. But it's a gray squirrel.

"When Gary touches the cake, I can sense its demise," my mother says. "Here's an idea. You take the top. And bring in the marzipan."

We've already unloaded everything else: the lace doilies, the water fountain, the napkins, etcetera. Landon and the guys left for the party two hours ago. The directions are in my purse. I know I can't go, but my urge to follow them to Ocean City hasn't subsided. The idea of Wick hooking up with Simone makes my vision blur.

I can't believe Landon was honest with me about that possibility. Doesn't he know that's the sort of thing I'm prone to obsess over? Does he have no twin connection with my sensibilities whatsoever? Why couldn't he have been a decent brother and lied?

Gary comes and stands beside me. I can feel his warmth, and smell his musky cologne. Why make a product designed to mimic the scent of an herbivorous furry land mammal that seldom bathes?

"You need help?" he asks. "I've got arms."

"I'm good," I say.

He takes off his suit jacket and drapes it over his shoulder, revealing his round belly.

"My brother is the groom," he says.

"Neat," I say, sounding way more enthusiastic than a normal person. I don't want to say anything offensive to the relative of a customer. When we get any sort of complaint on the comment cards, my mother freaks.

"At first they were going to go to the Bahamas for their honeymoon, but now they're headed to Virginia Beach. Financial limitations."

I stop unloading the cake and force myself to have a conversation with Gary-the-groomsman.

"I've heard good things about Virginia Beach," I say. I have never heard anything about Virginia Beach.

"Because of the storm they might delay it," Gary says. "They've got fluid arrangements with their hotel."

"That's the way to go," I say. If my future husband suggested taking me to Virginia Beach for our honeymoon with "fluid arrangements" for our hotel, I would ditch him at the altar. My parents honeymooned in Hawaii. Their photo album is packed with snapshots of them in swimsuits, standing next to palm trees, sipping on tall drinks decorated with colorful paper umbrellas and pineapple chunks. My mother said it was one of the best times of their marriage.

Gary winks at me. I guess he is interested in hitting on me after all. I bet it's the skirt. "You must love cake," he says. "Or are you around it so much that you hate it?"

"I like it."

"I could never be a baker. I'm a security guard. I guess we're all built with different engines." He points to his chest and makes a grinding noise. "I like risk."

I smile, and surrender the top tier of cake to him. "Cool."

"Everything okay?" my mother calls. I glance up the cement walkway to see her standing in the door.

"We're good," I say.

She's only a few car lengths away, but she looks so small. And worried.

"We should hurry," I say. "I'll get the marzipan."

Gary carefully slides his hand underneath the stiff cardboard rounder and balances the cake in the palm of his hand.

"Marzipan. So what's that stuff made out of? Paper pulp?"

I ignore him.

"Plaster of Paris? Eggs?"

"Nuts, Gary."

"Nuts?"

"Nuts," I repeat.

"Nice."

I offer no facial reaction.

"So, do you like to bowl?"

"Bowl?"

"Yeah, you do it with a ball. And your hand." Gary holds up his hand and stretches out his fingers.

"No," I say. "I have delicate hands." Two days ago getting asked out by Gary would have been an impossibility. I had a boyfriend. Now I'm an available person, and it's like he can smell it.

"They seem to get the job done," he says, pointing to the cake.

I swallow hard and look up into the sky. I have such little patience for polite chat. Everyone else in my family is great at it. My mother can converse about anything with anyone. Landon likes to pepper people with questions about their interests. And my father—well, he seems good at creating friends and lovers everywhere he goes. My father. I don't want to think about my father. I dread our upcoming conversation. There's got to be a way I can avoid it.

"How expensive would it be to rent a week in a youth hostel and just disappear for a while?"

"What?" he asks.

"Nothing. I was thinking out loud."

"If you want to talk hostels, I've crashed in a lot of

them. Find me inside. I'll give you the scoop," he says, winking at me again.

Gary walks off, and I study his vanishing figure. What are the chances that I'll end up with somebody like him? At first I think I'm asking myself a casual question. But the idea sticks. I watch the front door smack Gary on his butt as he kicks the rock we'd been using to prop open the main entrance. As he maneuvers himself inside, his jacket slides off his shoulder and gets caught in the door. Gary keeps going, leaving his suit jacket partway inside and partway outside. It's like his own clothing is trying to escape the fate of being worn by him.

I wonder how many types of men there are in the world. What happens if I let Wick go? What happens if I end up with a type Gary, a man who clocks in to his rent-a-cop job with soulful satisfaction?

I'm overreacting. I know that. There are more than two types of guys in the world. For instance, my father is nothing like Gary or Wick. He's gregarious and smart and athletic. If I could excise his impulse to carouse, he'd be almost perfect. I think back to when I was young and my father was actually perfect in my mind, before I knew the things I didn't want to know. Now he is a basement dweller. I think of his face. His voice. "Honey, we'll talk tonight."

I grab the box of marzipan from the back of the Subaru. I set it on the curb with such force that the cardboard flaps fly open. The wedding couple are wrapped in plastic and situated on the top. They have faces now, bright smiling, happy faces. Before I can think it through, I'm unwrapping them. What am I doing? Then it happens. Not because I want it to and not because I planned for it, but because sometimes things in life just happen.

I bite the shoes off the groom. It only takes one snap of my jaw, and I've got a wad of almond paste in my mouth. I chew it like I've been poisoned, and marzipan tuxedo shoes are the only antidote. At his pant cuffs I can see my smooth teeth marks.

Then I lift the bride to my mouth. I'm careful to take just her shoes and leave her delicate ankles intact. As I chew the marzipan, I try to swallow it fast. I want to digest it. I want it to become a part of me. I look at the de-footed bride. If you focus on her head, she doesn't really seem that different. But if you zero in on her ankles, she looks like she's been in some sort of unfortunate accident with a butter knife. I run my tongue along my teeth and smile. Take that, I think to the unnamed hordes of people out there who think I'm boring. I just did something crazy. I just did something stupid for no good reason at all. And I'm not finished either.

I don't try to mask my bite marks. I wrap the couple back up in the plastic and stick them in the box. Then I slam the trunk. The entranceway is empty. Everybody, including my mother, is tucked neatly inside the Sheraton. Now is my chance.

I pull the directions out of the purse. Ocean City is over 500 miles away. It would be insane to do this. I put the directions back inside my purse. But my life already

43

feels insane. I pull the directions back out. I'm ready to do something outside of what's expected of me. And I want to do this. Because I have a great reason. I love Wick Jarboe, and I can stop him from making the worst mistake of his life. I throw open the car door and get inside. The keys are still in the ignition. If I wasn't supposed to do this, the keys wouldn't be here. That's the rationale I use. All of the pieces have fallen into place. It's destiny.

It's after midnight when I pull onto the party block. I'm not sure what I'm supposed to do. I think I'll look bad, and by that I mean emotionally unbalanced, if I immediately storm the house and start making demands on Wick. I should probably case things out and try to catch him doing something wrong first. I drum my hands on the steering wheel and think this over.

I pick up my phone, which I muted outside Vergennes, and see that I've got fifteen missed calls from my mother, four from my father, and zero from Wick. Not even Landon has called me. I feel ridiculous. I toss the phone in the backseat.

My head throbs. The only thing I've eaten today is the marzipan shoes and a bag of pretzels that I bought at a gas station along the way. I'd intended to buy a sandwich, but their refrigeration system was down, and the only lunch-type food available was nachos. I couldn't bring myself to introduce a molten cheddar product into my mother's new car. Her bucket seats are so immaculate, they're virginal. Sadly, as much as I want to explore my risk-taking side, responsibility dominates my personality. Even while stealing a car.

I park down the street. What next? I've seen people stalk other people on television dramas. I replay those scenes. The next step now seems obvious. Hunched over, I run down the sidewalk through puddles of light made by the streetlamps overhead. For the first time in my life, I wish I was shorter than five feet four. After passing several well-groomed hedges, I finally arrive at 2510 Hobart. A dog barks at me from across the street.

I've already passed three signs alerting me that this street is protected by a Neighborhood Watch. I wonder if I look suspicious? A car passes by and I hurry into the back.

Before I round the corner, I hear all their voices. They're sitting in the backyard. I stay on the side of the house and crouch down in the grass.

Burr: "She wants you."

Dale: "Dude, I know. She gave me two phone numbers. Her cell and her home."

Burr: "It's almost desperate."

Landon: "She didn't look desperate. She looked limber."

[Burr unleashes a howl that sounds like an excited dog.]

Dale: "I know! How many Olympic gymnasts can a guy expect to meet in his life? Zero. I'm totally going to call her."

Wick: "When?"

Dale: "I'll wait three days. You always wait three days."

Munny: "You'll be back in Vermont in three days. Maybe you should truncate your wait period."

Dale: "I'll truncate you."

Landon: "Munny makes a good point. Why not just call her tomorrow?"

Dale: "Maybe."

Burr: "Live a little. She's a *gymnast*. She's peaking right now. You'll never get another shot like this."

Dale: "Dude, Skate, you haven't washed your hand yet, right?"

Skate: "Trust your wingman. Seven digits on this hand. Seven digits on this one. So even if I lose one of my hands, you'll still have her number."

Dale: "Cool."

Sov: "Seven? Don't you need her area code too?"

Dale: "Shit. Do you have her area code?"

Skate: "I've got that memorized. Four, four, three."

Dale: "Don't forget that. This could turn into something."

Sov: "What's her name?"

Dale: "Um."

Wick: "You forgot her name already?"

Dale: "Shit."

Burr: "Concentrate on what she was wearing, and maybe it will come back to you."

Dale: "Skirt. Nice legs. Funky belt. She could actually lose the belt. A little too bohemian for me. Rack was decent. Natalie! Her name is Natalie."

Burr: "Good recall."

Dale: "Yeah. That was a boner-sustaining moment for me."

I hear the sound of a can cracking open. I'm disgusted. If somebody says all of the digits in Natalie-the-gymnast's phone number, I am going to call her and warn her about Dale.

Burr: "If I weren't Mormon, I think I'd own a bar."

Landon: "Yeah, I've noticed that your faith totally seems to be stifling your lifestyle."

Burr: "And my future."

Dale: "It would be awesome if you owned a bar. What would you name it?"

Burr: "The Thirsty Manatee."

Dale: "I'd drink there."

Munny: "If you don't want to be Mormon, why don't you quit? Take your life into your own hands while you're still young."

[Long pause.]

Skate: "It's our heritage. It's who we are."

Landon: "Let's not get too serious."

Wick: "I came for a party."

Dale: "Dude, the Thirsty Manatee? Have you ever seen a manatee?"

Skate: "Yeah, I've ridden Jet Skis off the coast of Florida. They're everywhere. Like aquatic deer."

Dale: "What the hell are aquatic deer?"

Sov: "He's saying that they're plentiful."

Munny: "Jet Skis maim lots of sea life, manatees in particular."

Dale: "You've confused me for somebody who cares about the ass of a manatee."

Munny: "You're right."

Wick: "This doesn't really feel like a party."

Landon: "Yeah, it's like I'm watching *National Geographic*."

Skate: "Let's drink."

Burr: "Bring it."

Landon: "Hold the fort. I'm going to grab a jacket."

Dale: "Grab mine too. Hey. Maybe we should start a fire."

Burr: "We don't have a pit."

Dale: "Minor setback. We could make one. And there's a ton of wood around this place."

Wick: "Why don't we put on jackets and wait to burn down the world until tomorrow night."

Skate: "That works."

Wick is so sensible. It's one of his best qualities. But he's got a lot of good qualities. One of my favorites is that he's completely tuned in to other people. Once, to cheer me up, he made an amazing picnic lunch for me in Leddy Park. I'd just gotten a terrible grade on an English paper about *Animal Farm*. I tried to locate redeeming qualities in Squealer. Wick used a pig-shaped cookie cutter to mold a variety of cheeses into all the swine characters from the book. I ate those symbolic pigs and laughed harder than I'd ever laughed with another person.

I lean back against the house and try to will my head not to ache. At the rate things are going, it could take hours before Wick does anything incriminating.

"Man, look at the moon," Skate says. "It looks just like a lemon wedge. I feel like I should write a poem about that moon."

Based on the e-zine, I'm not sure if Skate has poet potential. Is he sincere enough? Can he make his rhymes less lazy? Stop. Why am I being so mean? This is one of the last times I'll be around him before he goes to college. Maybe my mother is right. Maybe I'm pushing him and Burr away. We don't talk at all anymore. And we stopped talking way before the e-zine incident. I didn't know how to handle things. I'd never lost anybody before. I was worried I'd say the wrong thing.

"Write a poem about this moon," Dale says.

I hear the sound of a zipper followed by the clink of a belt buckle hitting the pavement. Laughter erupts. I don't need to see what's happening. Wick's brother is notorious for mooning people, places, and things. Once, after pressing his pasty cheeks against the emergency exit window on the way home from school—as we passed an outdoor church brunch for widows—Dale was permanently banned from the school bus.

I begin to pluck at the grass. I keep expecting to hear Simone's dumb giggle float around the corner. But it truly seems to be a gathering of just guys. I'm ashamed. I didn't do anything interesting; I just did something incredibly stupid. I guess it's a fine line between the two. How will I explain things to my mother? What excuse can I possibly come up with for abandoning her and putting more than a thousand extra miles on her new car? I guess I can claim an illness. Like I thought my appendix was bursting, and I wanted to get to a really good hospital that specialized in that sort of thing. Or maybe I should keep thinking.

But thinking makes me feel like throwing up. In a patch of wet grass, I lie down. I can't listen to them drink beer and eat pizza all night. Shouldn't I drive back? A charley horse is starting in my calf. I stand and hop on my right leg, trying to unkink the muscle in my left. Sadly, pumps are not a tight-fitting shoe. I watch the left shoe sail in the direction of the guys. I hunker down in the grass again. My shoe is not in clear view; it's off to the side, still hidden in the darkness. But it's so white it looks somewhat radioactive. Somebody drags a chair across the cement patio.

"Well, boys, I think it's time we visit Gretchen."

The gathering seems happy about this suggestion. More metal chair legs rub across the patio. Cheers and whistles mix with the unpleasant scraping sound.

"I'll get more beer," offers Burr.

"Who's going to drive?" asks Sov. "You can't drink and drive in my dad's van."

I feel a little sorry for Sov and Munny. Sometimes I think Burr uses them. Dale too. Sov and Munny's dad works as the assistant men's basketball coach for the University of Vermont. They get free tickets to games and the chance to mingle with the players. Sometimes they share these perks with their friends. It's pretty obvious that the guys enjoy basking in the cultural cachet that Mr. Paddington's job extends to them. Sov and Munny aren't too caught up in it, but Burr, Skate, and Dale love it.

Sov and Munny don't care about college sports. Their extracurricular interests are global and fall into two camps: political science and literature. Sov and Munny run this after-school group called the Culture Club, and it attracts all sorts of popular kids: cheerleaders, football players, drama freaks, class officers, the tennis team, stoners, etcetera. They read books. Mainly about philosophy and other cultures, I think. And they also eat foods that represent the philosophical idea or culture that they're reading about.

And the Culture Club has some pull. Both Robert Pinsky and George Saunders have written the club letters, declining (due to scheduling conflicts and lack of payment) to come and take part in discussions about their books. Their missives are short, but pretty polite. Sov and Munny got permission to hang the letters in the trophy case. You'd think the Culture Club would be a gathering of losers, but it's totally the opposite. The month they read Hélène Cixous and ate crepes, I strongly considered going.

"Seriously, Burr," Sov says. "No beer in the van. I'm not losing interstate road tripping privileges for you."

I wish I had those kinds of privileges.

"Suit yourself, boys," adds Skate. "But Gretchen feels better after a few beers." He laughs. Burr howls like a dog again. Landon joins him. I stick my finger down my throat and pretend to gag myself. I don't think I'll ever be able to think like a guy. I have way too many brain cells. I pull my finger out of my mouth and wait to hear Wick say that he doesn't want to visit Gretchen. But Wick isn't voicing any dissent.

"I think we should leave the beer here," says Sov. "If any of it spills in the van, my dad will be able to smell it."

Burr laughs. "Relax. We won't drive with open containers. We're law abiders."

Is he trying to be ironic? They're drinking underage. I wonder if Sov and Munny will stand their ground. Maybe they'll act like moral anchors and keep the rest of the guys from becoming reckless idiots. Sov and Munny are the youngest among the twin group. I suspect the main reason they were invited to the party is because their father was willing to lend the guys their fifteen-passenger van. Of course, Sov and Munny didn't drive; they're only fifteen. The other five probably took turns, unlike me, who had to be woman enough to do it on her own.

"More beer for me," Burr says.

This sound of his voice makes me shiver. Why does he need to act like this? Has his grief turned him into an exaggerated rebel? And what's wrong with his uncle? How can you buy your bereaved nephews beer? Who does that? Apparently somebody who is not concerned with contributing to the delinquency of a minor. And what about Gretchen? Who's Gretchen? She sounds like a floozy. She might be a friend of Simone's. The guys seem very excited to get to her. For all I know, she could be an exotic dancer. If she is, I bet she's the kind who takes it all off.

Wick: "My battery's dead. Anyone have a phone I can use? I need to send a text."
Dale: "I'm not surprised. You were on that thing the whole way down."
Landon: "Here. I'll text for ya. Whoa. My mom's called five times."
Wick: "She loves you."
Dale: "Do you need to call Mama?"
Landon: "It can wait. I told her I'd check in Sunday."

I hold my breath. My life is a crisis. I don't want Landon to talk to Mom, and who was Wick talking to? Wick doesn't spend countless hours on the phone. I stare at Wick's phone as though it's going to be capable of giving me answers. Maybe Wick is going to text me. Where is my phone? It's in the Subaru. The suspense of waiting until I get back to my car to check makes me feel unusually vulnerable. The wind picks up, and I clench my jaw to keep my teeth from chattering.

When the guys finally go inside, I move toward my shoe. I grab it quickly. It's the first sense of relief I've felt in a long time. I start to creep back to my car. On the way, I can't resist peeking into a side window of the house. This place is a total pigsty. Burr and Skate's uncle must be a bachelor. The guys are moving around in the kitchen. There's a lot of empty pizza boxes on the floor. Near the refrigerator, I can see the back of Landon's head. Sometimes, when I look at his face, I think I can see the outline of my own features: thin nose, pointed chin. Not now. His dark hair has reformed its curls, and they're shooting out in every direction, and he looks agitated. Clearly, this is not the party of the century. I feel a little bit better knowing this.

Whether or not I continue to trail the guys all depends on what I find when I finally reach my phone. Once inside my car, I am devastated by what I find. There is no text from Wick. I see additional calls from my parents, and toss the phone in the backseat again. I need to trail the guys. I don't know what I'll do when I get to Gretchen's, but I have to follow them. I love Wick. Even if we're on a break. Even if he doesn't text me. I want to make sure that he's loyal. Because a break shouldn't mean that you get to travel out of state and start hooking up with anybody you want. A break means that you stay home and play reflective music and stew over the person you broke away from.

Doesn't he get that? Doesn't anybody in that stupid group of guys understand how a heart works? I know they don't read romance novels, but haven't they seen a movie or two about it? Women need to be reassured. Women need to feel cared about. Women need men in their lives who treat them like they matter.

I watch them climb into the van, completely unaware that I'm here. All of them are accommodating Burr and Skate. The group never had ringleaders before. The power was spread evenly. Even I had power. But it's not like that anymore. The tragedy shifted everything. Burr and Skate, on the heels of their exodus from Vermont, are acting macho and reckless. Burr more than Skate. Burr could ask the guys to do anything and they'd agree. Grief has cast a spell on them.

The van cruises right by my car. Wick is driving, and he doesn't even see me. His mouth is moving. It looks like he's singing along to the radio. He appears absolutely happy. I feel completely betrayed. How can Wick be happy? How is that possible? I pull out and follow the guys. I want him to prove to me that he's not anything like my father. I want Wick to show me that I made the right decision to love him. And that everything between us is going to be okay.

chapter 6

The guys drive toward the coast. I glide down a small hill and notice how the twinkling lights of the city abruptly end; the water spreads out beyond the land like a dark blanket. It's chilly out. Even though it's August, I flip on the heater. I didn't dress appropriately for a reconnaissance mission. I should have brought a jacket. Man-catching attire and spy attire are two totally separate fashion statements.

The guys race through two yellow lights and roll through a four-way stop. Didn't they listen to the radio on the way down? Didn't they see the jackknifed truck near Wilmington? I did. Police lights. Ambulance sirens. Fire truck. Seeing mangled metal on the freeway should slow down their full-throttle approach to life. The news report on the radio said that the driver had been critically injured. I got there right as everything was being cleared. But they could have been there right after it happened. Doesn't hearing about that stuff make the guys feel frail?

I bet that it made Wick feel frail. He's one of the most emotional guys in the van. This isn't something I suspect simply because we've dated. There's scientific data supporting it. All of us have had our emotional reactions tested in the twin studies. I wonder if Wick has thought about what it's going to feel like going to twin studies as a broken-up couple? The testers might figure out a way to incorporate our situation into one of their experiments. The thought of this makes me feel even more panicked. I don't want my heartache documented by university researchers.

Wick and Dale's mother works in the psychology department at the University of Vermont. So does Sov and Munny's mother. It's their mothers who started the group. The Jarboes have lived within walking distance of our house since before Landon and I were born. When we turned eight, my parents approached Landon and me with the chance to be part of a study for twins. It was supposed to help collect information about twin responses. And our participation would be compensated with contributions to a college fund. At that age, I didn't understand the importance of a college fund. But I did like the idea of meeting other twins. I was brokenhearted when it turned out that I was the only girl.

Once a month, on Fridays, for the past eight years, Sov, Munny, Wick, Dale, Burr, Skate, Landon, and I have participated in twin studies. Usually, they separate us from our respective twins and have us fill out questionnaires, or eat interesting foods, or play games; they've even poked us on various parts of our bodies. The whole point is to test the psychic connection between twins.

Landon and I are the least connected twins. Burr and Skate are the most. If you prick Burr's finger, Skate can feel it. If you make Skate watch a sad movie, Burr, seated in another room, will suddenly be moved to tears. Not Landon and me. If you show him a picture of a circle and ask me what he's looking at, I say a square. If you have me smell a banana, and ask him what fruit he's craving, he'll say a peach. If you ask me to think of a letter and have him guess it, we'll usually be as far apart as two letters can get. Once I was thinking of the letter *Q* and he guessed the letter *E*. He said he was responding to a feeling he was experiencing concerning the schwa sound. Sometimes I can guess Landon. But it's hit and miss.

When we arrive at the marina, I see that the parking stalls have yellow numbers spray-painted on each one. I know that this means that they're probably assigned, and that if I park there, I risk getting a ticket or possibly towed. But in matters of love, isn't a tow worth the risk?

I scan the parking lot for someone who looks like a Gretchen. But there's no one. The guys climb out of the van and make their way toward the boats tied to the docks. I don't know much about boats. These look big, like yachts, like you could maybe live on them. The guys are laughing. Under an arm, Skate and Burr are each carrying a brown paper sack. I can't believe that they're both going to attend Brigham Young University in the fall. Maybe that's the whole point of drinking now. Once they enter Utah, they won't be getting inebriated again for quite some time.

I hide behind cars, keeping about a hundred yards between me and them. My heart is racing. I glance back at my mother's Subaru. I parked it in stall seven, because seven is a lucky number. I still don't see Gretchen. Maybe she's waiting for them on one of the boats. I consider leaving the guys here and turning back. I keep going back and forth.

Enid, you've come this far, keep following them.

Enid, you've lost your mind. Go home.

Enid, next time you do something like this, wear better shoes and bring binoculars.

Enid, what really brought you here: Wick? The llama? Your broken heart? Gary? The rubber-band principle? The story of Moses? Your father?

I'm so confused. And tired. Stalking requires a ton of mental energy. And muscle strength. My thighs quake from supporting me in a crouched position. It's time to return to Vermont. But who is Gretchen? I can't leave until I know. Once I know, I'll leave.

"Can I help you?" a voice asks.

I almost scream. I look over my shoulder and see a middle-aged man and a girl about my age peering down at me.

"What do you mean?" I ask.

"This is my car," he says.

"Your car?"

He points aggressively at the silver Lexus in front of me.

He has a vanity plate. It says RNIXON.

"R. Nixon?" I ask.

"Yes, Rich Nixon. It's a family name."

Because I've been caught off guard, I remain crouched.

It takes me a couple of seconds to realize that I'm gripping Rich Nixon's back bumper. People dislike it when other people touch their cars, especially with both hands. I'm so scared I feel like I'm going to wet myself.

"Do you need a bathroom?" he asks.

I turn bright red. He thinks that I was trying to pee next to his car.

"I've lost my car," I say. I'm standing now, trying to look totally normal. I tug at my blouse and smooth it over my stomach.

"There's only six cars in the lot," he says, sweeping his arm around, gesturing to the other vehicles.

I'm certain that I look incredibly suspicious, and realize my best option is to lie my way out of this.

"My brother parked the car, and I'm trying to find it," I say. I can't believe how good that sounded.

The girl points to my key ring. "Can't you just press that button?"

She means the UNLOCK button. "Good idea," I say. "I'll try that."

Rich Nixon and the girl keep looking at me. They want me to try it now. So I do.

The Subaru's headlights flash on and off.

"It's over there," the girl says.

"Thanks a bunch," I say.

"You're from Vermont?" he asks, pointing to my car's green license plate.

"Yes."

"Long ways from home."

"I know. I'm headed home right now."

"Travel safely," the girl says.

They watch me walk to the car and I climb inside. They get inside their Lexus. I start my car. They drive off. I try looking around the parking lot, but all I see is my own hair. It's exploded. This has never happened to me before, and I suspect this condition has been brought on not only by the humidity but also by my nerves.

I dig around in the glove box in hopes of finding a rubber band. Because it's a new car, I know my chances of finding anything useful are slim, but my mother is quite a clutter bug. There's a ton of paperwork. And a pair of mittens, which makes no sense, and one of my dad's baseball caps. As I pull my hair back and slip on the cap, I realize that it smells exactly like my father. Can I stand to wear a hat that smells like him? I take it off.

In the very back of the glove box, I find a small white gift box. Opening it up, I find a wide silver barrette resting on top of a thin sheet of cotton stuffing. It's new. On the inside of the box lid are the words: "I can make it up to you." It's my father's handwriting. He thinks gifts can make up for everything. I take the barrette and throw it at the windshield, but it ricochets off the glass and lands in my lap. Catching a glimpse of myself in the rearview mirror, I know I can't continue to stalk Wick while sporting such freaky and uncontrollable hair. I sweep my bangs and long sides into the metal clip and snap it shut.

With my reinstated peripheral vision, I scan the parking lot again. The guys aren't anywhere. They've escaped. I'm so mad that I hit the steering wheel. Then I think about Rich Nixon and the girl, and I get so angry that I scream. She probably wasn't even his daughter. I bet the jerk is cheating on his wife.

I shake off the encounter and look at the empty gift box. My choices don't feel real. Turn around and drive to Vermont and face my screwed-up life? Or go forward and face the complete unknown? Before I realize it, I'm out of the car. But I can't run anymore in these heels; I'm developing a blister. Worse than that, my pantyhose are already giving me thigh rash. They keep slipping. I slide them down my hips. I forgot that I'm wearing orange underwear. I leave the balled-up hose beside the car. I'm done with them.

The lot is completely void of people, and this makes my quest feel dire. Where did the guys go? I move toward the boats. Waves lick against their wooden and fiberglass sides. I could go right or left. The plank dock extends in both directions. The thought of losing them terrifies me. Should I go left or right?

Out of nowhere comes a howl. It's Burr. And his howl came from the left. I run down the dock, head held high, trying to step as lightly as I can.

There's no sign of Gretchen, but I see the guys. They're on a boat, and it's big, almost as long as a school bus. The guys are seated on the front end of it, which is the end farthest from the dock. They're laughing. Beer cans are cracking open. Even though it might not be the best idea, I move to the back of the boat and jump the railing, dropping down onto the deck. I make a thumping sound, and the boat rocks. Plus, I skinned my knee.

The laughing stops, and I can hear footsteps moving toward me. I scamper through a doorway and crawl down four steep steps. There's a kitchen down here. And a bed. And a closet. No, when I open the door I can see a toilet. It's a bathroom. I get inside and close the door.

"I don't see anything," Wick says. "It must be the wind."

"Check below," Burr hollers.

"It was the wind," Wick says.

"Sometimes people board ships and rob them. It's happened before," explains Burr.

The floor squeaks as Wick comes down the stairs.

"Hello?" he calls. "Any criminals down here? Thieves in particular? Or persons of interest in unsolved homicide cases?"

In spite of everything, I can't help but smile. I really like Wick's sense of humor. I think it's, like, thirty-three percent of the reason I find him so stalkable. I silently beg him not to open the door. I doubt he'd find being stalked across state lines a funny situation. He'd probably get all taken aback or outraged or frightened. But really, my following him down here and hiding in this bathroom is a total compliment. It's a testament to both my love and his desirability. I hold my breath and sit down on the toilet.

"Drop your weapons if you're armed," he says.

I hear him open a cupboard in the kitchen.

"I'm packing heat!" a voice yells.

The voice is low. I'm not sure who this person is.

Somebody knocks against the bathroom door and falls onto the floor.

"Real funny, Burr. I could've been hurt," Wick says.

"Are you nuts? You can't ask criminals to surrender themselves. You've got to take them by surprise," Burr says.

Burr is laughing. I hear them walking up the stairs.

"It was the wind," Wick repeats.

"I guess," Burr says. "But what about the creaking?"

"She's a wooden ship," Wick says. "Of course she's going to creak. How long have you owned *Gretchen* anyway?"

"My parents got her ten years ago," Burr says.

"Oh," Wick says.

I think the tone in Wick's *oh* sounds sad. I can feel a shift in energy. Normally, Wick would have a fun comeback. He and Burr would banter, and because Wick is smarter and cleverer, he'd pull off the better zingers and wind up on top. A dude version of bonding. But since the accident, Wick handles Burr differently. He pulls back. He doesn't use comebacks. He absorbs Burr's jokes and laughs at them. Funny or not.

"It's a nice boat," Wick finally says.

"Too bad it can't come to Utah," Burr says. "I could have my own chick frigate."

Wick laughs again.

They're so far away now that I can't clearly hear the conversation anymore. And then their voices are completely gone. I lean my head against a towel hanging on the wall. It's monogrammed: RMR. Skate and Burr's mother's name was Robin Marie Riggs. It sucks that a towel can outlast a person. It shouldn't be this way. I pull the towel down and fold it four times, trying to make a pillow. The towel smells like the Riggses' house, so I press my face into the terry cloth and breathe deeply. Even six months after their deaths, it's still so shocking. Until they were killed, whenever I heard of people dying in planes, I always pictured crashes. Airliners plummeting from the sky into marshy areas. Or slamming into snowcapped mountains. But that's not what happened to Mr. and Mrs. Riggs. They hadn't even taken off yet. The plane was sitting on the tarmac in Boston, and they were in their seats aboard a flight bound for San Diego. They were on their way to celebrate their twentieth anniversary. But as the plane taxied down the runway, one of the engines exploded, and debris ripped through the cabin.

Burr and Skate's parents were the only people who died. Their wounds must have been massive, because the funeral was closed-casket. It was so surreal. Burr spoke. Skate sobbed. I wore a black pantsuit, sat still, and repeated over and over again: *This is part of life, this is part of life.* But this strategy did little to help me get on top of my sadness. I felt clobbered by despair. I kept looking in disbelief at the Riggses' caskets. They were inside of them. People I'd known my whole life—*people I loved*—were dead. At one point, I heard a man sitting one pew ahead of me whisper into another man's ear that it had been a blessing that the Riggses were taken together and so quickly.

I find it hard to characterize being mortally wounded while seated in coach class on a commercial airliner the day before your twentieth anniversary as anything other than a tragedy. I mean, they orphaned their twin boys. I can't imagine what that feels like, to be a teenager and an orphan. Most of the time, I feel totally lost, and I've got two parents. Okay, so they're both pretty flawed. But I have them.

Mr. and Mrs. Riggs's deaths shook everyone. My impulsive father even went out and bought an expensive life insurance policy the very next week. My mother started taking me out to lunch at fancy restaurants every other Thursday. The night of the funeral, Landon came into my room. He stood in my doorway blotchy-faced and crying. He just stared at me.

I said, "I know how you feel."

He said, "No, you don't."

Then he told me that he loved me. He said I was the most important person in his life. I remember not being sure if that was true. I'm still not sure. Other people dying has that effect on you. It makes you feel panicked, and depressed, and grateful, all at once.

The smell of the Riggses' house is starting to make me feel nauseated. I put the towel in the corner farthest from me. I need to figure out how to get out of this bathroom.

I see a little lock shaped like a small button on the door, and I press it down. It makes me feel better, like I'll have some warning before I get caught. God, I hope I can get off this boat without getting caught. I can't think of a good reason to explain why I'm in this tiny bathroom. Right now I feel very doomed. *Gretchen* isn't even a stripper. It's just the name of this dumb boat.

The guys can't stay here forever. Once they leave, I'll leave. Problem solved. I keep trying to get comfortable, but the Subaru keys dig into my skin near my hip bone. They've clawed a hole in my skirt pocket, which annoys me to no end. I hate damaging borrowed goods. I take the keys out of my pocket and set them on the sink next to a small rectangle of soap. The shabby beige bar looks like the kind that you get for free in hotels. When I think of hotels, I think of the Sheraton and my mother, whom I should never have left. I feel like crying. If anyone opens this door, I'm going to look like that stereotypical teenage girl who has a public meltdown and loses her mind. The one who spends her entire high school existence trying to live down her reputation for being freaky. But she never quite gets there.

chapter 7

Time has passed, but I'm not sure how much. I fell asleep, sitting right here on the can. Miniature bottles of shampoo and conditioner are scattered at my feet. The car keys have slid into the sink's bowl along with the beige soap. Waves must rock ships even when they're tied to the dock. I reach to pick up the bottles, but the ship jerks and they slide out of my grasp. I also lose my balance and fall onto the floor.

"The door's locked," Sov states loudly. "I can't get it open."

I reseat myself on the toilet. This isn't good news.

"Pee off the side," Dale says.

I'm surprised by that suggestion, because the other boats in the marina are so close to this one; it seems indecent. But then again, it's Dale's suggestion, and when it comes to decency, he lacks a lot.

"I'm not pissing in the Atlantic in this storm," Sov says.

"Dude, if you fall in, I'll personally toss you a life preserver," Dale says. "You know how to dog-paddle, right?"

They must be standing in the kitchen area, because I can hear them just fine.

"There's sharks," Sov says.

This makes no sense to me. We're in the harbor; we're not in the Atlantic.

"Pee off the side or hold it. I'm not going to jimmy the lock when I've already given you a better solution." I hear Dale climb the stairs, and his voice grows softer. "Burr and Skate want to watch the sunrise from the water."

That sucks. This means that the ship is actually out to sea. That I'm actually out to sea. Now there's no sneaking off. I'm here. I'm stuck on this thing until morning. And Sov is going to pee himself and it's all my fault.

The boat jerks again. I can't let Sov wet himself. Or risk falling into the Atlantic. Even though it's completely stupid of me, I decide to open the door.

"Sov," I whisper. "Sov, come here."

He stands before me in flip-flops, jeans, and a pale yellow polo shirt.

"What are you doing here?" he asks. "Why are you so dressed up? What's wrong with your hair?"

"Keep your voice down," I say. I reach out, grab hold of his arm, and ignore the hair question. Hasn't he ever heard of humidity? "Listen, I came from a wedding. I realize that I'm overdressed. You can come in here and use the toilet, but you can't tell anyone that I'm here, okay?"

"Are you here to see Wick? Is this about your breakup?" Sov asks.

"So, he's mentioned it?" I ask. "Did he call it a breakup or did he say we were on a break? Because there's a huge difference between those two things."

"Enid, I have to pee."

"Okay, but don't tell Wick I'm here. I drove down because I thought I had some things I wanted to discuss with him, but I've rethought it. Once we dock, I plan to leave and wait to talk to him back in Vermont."

"Good idea," he says.

I nod.

"Okay," he says. "But I can't use it with you in here." He's biting his bottom lip and he looks like he's in pain.

"Yeah, but where do you want me to go?" I ask. "I need to stay hidden."

He twists out of my grasp and turns around. I think it's over, that my cover is blown. Instead, he comes back holding a wicker clothes hamper.

"Hide in here," he says.

I look at it and know immediately that I'm too tall to fit.

"I'll cover you with this," he says, holding up a sheet. "We'll put you in the corner. I need to use the toilet and I won't pee in the Atlantic. That's dangerous."

I hurry out of the bathroom and bang my shin on a bolted-down chair. I pick up the hamper and move it to the corner next to the full-size bed and climb in. Sov hands me a pillow and tosses a sheet over me.

"Thanks, Enid. I won't tell anyone."

Sov enters the bathroom and shuts the door. I feel like a decent human being for putting him out of his suffering. The wicker pokes through my shirt, and scrapes against my bare legs. Also, my left ankle is wrenched into an unnatural and painful position. I would make a lousy magician's assistant.

Sov exits the bathroom and thanks me again.

I lift my head out of the hamper, like a slow-moving jack-in-the-box, and tell him, "No problem."

After he's gone, I settle back down. As I sit in the hamper I contemplate which is worse: getting caught in the bathroom, or being discovered scrunched-up in the dirty clothes basket. Each one comes with its own distinct humiliation. I'm getting ready to crawl out of the hamper and retreat to the toilet again, when the boat jerks suddenly, knocking the hamper over.

I clunk onto the floor, banging my head pretty hard. The ship lunges the other way—violently—and I feel like I'm going to be sick.

"Jesus! Skate, we need to go back to shore," Landon yells.

I know things are serious. I've never heard Landon yell like that before. Because I don't know what to do, I stay on the ground halfway inside the hamper. The boat keeps rolling me around on the floor. I can't control where my body goes. I knock into every wall, and things from the kitchen cupboards begin to shower down on me. Glass jars break open. A coffee can topples onto my head, and the plastic lid pops off, caking my hair in a dark, bitter powder.

Upstairs, the wind is howling. I can hear the guys yelling at each other. I crawl off the floor and sit on the bed. It's cold, and the air is thick with mist. I feel very

71

alone. Maybe I should go upstairs. Does it matter if I get caught? The boat lurches up and down. It feels like we're free-falling from one tall wave to the next. One plunge is so bad, I actually slam against the ceiling, banging the barrette into my scalp.

As I hold my aching head, I see water begin to tumble down the stairs. This is hard for me to process. It feels like I must be dreaming. I don't know why, but I reach down and take off my shoes. I hold them close to me. I don't want to lose them. They're my mother's.

"We're okay," Burr yells. "She's a big ship."

I hear Wick cry out. But I can't make out the words that he's saying. The muddled sounds make my skin goose-pimple and the hair on the back of my neck stand up. Burr and Skate are ordering the guys around, telling them to do things with the sails. Dale must be the one steering the ship. I haven't heard Sov or Munny say anything. I hope they weren't knocked overboard. Water continues to flow down the stairs. It mixes with all the crud that's been spilled on the floor, resulting in a nasty-looking soup. How much water can a ship hold? Should I find a bucket and try to bail with it? Is that what people do in situations like this? I stay seated on the bed, hugging my shoes, and continue to watch the water level rise. This is the most interesting thing that has ever happened to me. And I hate it.

"I'll check on that," Skate yells.

The next thing I know, I'm looking at his shoes, legs, and body as he rushes down below. As he's climbing down the stairs, he slips and his legs fly out from underneath him. He crashes into the soup.

"Skate?" I say. I jump off the bed and crawl to his side. I worry that the reason he slipped is because he saw me and was startled.

His head hit the edge of the bottom stair. He's bleeding.

"Help!" I yell. "We need bandages."

I hear someone running down the stairs.

"They're slick," I cry. "Be careful."

I glance up and see Wick hovering above us. He looks very surprised, and I don't offer an explanation.

"Enid?" he asks.

"Skate is hurt," I say. "Where's the first-aid kit?"

"I don't know," he says.

"Find out," I say.

"It's not that bad," Skate says.

"You're bleeding," I say. I focus on Skate. I tune out the chaos. I have a job. Fix Skate's wound.

"I've taken worse falls," Skate says. "Remember that picnic near Quechee Gorge? Way worse."

"You fell down a gorge?" Wick asks.

I shake my head. "Out of a tree." I take the sheet that had been used to cover me and rip it into strips.

"I'll find a first-aid kit," Wick says.

"It was so obvious the oak could never support that much weight."

"It *became* obvious," Skate whispers.

When I start wrapping the strips around Skate's head, he breathes in a quick gasp of air. Then his eyes clap closed, and he pushes me away.

"She's trying to help," Wick says. He's returned with the first-aid kit and Dale.

"What's going on up there?" I ask.

"It's a storm. Dude, the waves are huge," Dale says.

"Who's steering us?" I ask. I'd assumed it was Dale.

"Landon," Wick says.

"*What?* He doesn't know how to steer a ship," I shout. "This is the third time he's ever been on a boat."

"Somebody has to be the captain. Burr is trying to fix the sails," Dale replies.

"Why did you guys go out to sea?" I ask. "This is so stupid."

Wick shakes his head. He's applied some rubbing alcohol to Skate's wound and is trying to tighten the bandage.

"Enid, what are you doing here?" Wick asks.

I don't answer.

"He needs to be on the bed. Let's move him," Wick says to Dale.

"I can do it," Skate says.

But I'm not sure that he can. He face looks flushed. His eyes are unfocused. And he doesn't seem capable of standing up. He attempts to sit, but he lies back down. Together Wick and Dale scoop Skate up and lower him onto the bare mattress.

"Thanks," Skate says.

"He seems so out of it," I say.

"He needs water," Wick says. "He's been drinking all night."

74

"Why did you let him do that?" I ask.

Wick ignores my question. The sloppy sea sloshes around my ankles.

"There's a cooler on deck," Wick says. "It has water in it."

I look up the stairs.

"I don't want Landon to know I'm here."

Dale looks at me like I'm the unbalanced teen stalker that I don't want to feel like. "I think the cat's out of the bag," he says.

I shake my head again.

"Enid and Dale, this is an emergency," Wick snaps. Normally, Wick moves through the world with confidence and optimism. But as I stare at him now, I'm looking at something else. I might as well be looking into Dale's uncertain and frustrated face.

"Okay," I say. "I know."

"Let's get him some water!" Wick yells.

I don't move. Dale rushes past me up the stairs. I look at Skate. The blood has already saturated the bandage.

"Should we call the Coast Guard?" I ask.

"I'm okay," Skate says softly.

"I don't know how to call the Coast Guard," Wick says.

The boat pitches to the right, and Wick and I fall on top of each other in the floor's gross swill.

"There's glass," I say. I've cut my hand. The pain feels hot, and I hope it's not too serious. Wick pulls me to him and my head bumps into his mouth.

"Why do you smell like a cappuccino?" he asks.

"I think it's a combination of my conditioner and that," I say, pointing to a large floating tin of Maxwell House. The boat jerks again, knocking us away from each other. As I crawl toward him, one of my shoes floats by.

"You came in heels?" he asks.

"I came from a wedding."

"Why are you here?" he asks again.

I don't know if I'm supposed to answer him. I can feel myself wanting to cry. I think I'm in shock. The situation around me makes no sense and I don't know how to process it.

"You shouldn't be here. This is crazy," he says.

"I thought 'Gretchen' was a stripper."

"You followed us from Vermont?" he asks.

I close my eyes. Tears roll down my cheeks, and I hear myself say, "I know. I wish I hadn't come."

chapter 8

By the time Dale returns, the area below deck is flooded with over a foot of water. Instead of bottled water, Dale is holding a can of Sprite. I'm sitting with Wick on the bed next to Skate. He keeps drifting in and out.

When Wick sees the can of Sprite, he balls up his fist and punches the bed. Skate groans.

"He needs water; he's dehydrated."

"I did the best I could. I didn't see any water. Sprite's better than Coke, right?"

Wick refuses to take the can. He gets up and cautiously wades to the counter.

"There's nothing in there," I say. "Everything's already spilled."

Wick opens a cupboard and finds some stuff wedged in the back. He begins emptying it out, pulling random cans and jars onto the floor.

"Dude, you're making a mess," Dale says.

"Shut up with the 'dudes,'" Wick yells. "This is serious."

I like that Wick is taking charge. Better him calling the shots than Dale.

Skate groans again and I touch his arm. A thin line of blood winds down a crease in his neck, staining his skin and collar an awful red.

"It's fine," Skate says.

Things do not feel fine.

"Have you guys ever been out in a storm this bad?" I ask.

Skate closes his eyes. "It'll be fine. Burr will figure this out."

The wind and water bang against the ship. It feels like we're caught in a disaster. And I don't think of Burr as a natural-born savior.

I'm holding Skate's hand. He gives mine a squeeze, but it's not very tight. Absorbed into the sheets, his blood looks so bright.

"You're going to be okay," I say. "Wick's getting you some water."

The muscles in Skate's face relax when I tell him this. The boat won't stay steady; it jostles us in every possible direction.

"Here," Wick says, holding up a small bottle of spring water.

I turn to Skate and tell him that we found some water. He smiles. Wick struggles to stay standing and returns to the bed. He sits down and unscrews the cap.

"You'll feel better now," Wick tells him. "Sobriety will improve everything."

Skate barely has a chance to swallow before the boat throws us up in the air. It's the worst wave yet. We all land in a jumble on the bed, and I hear a crash behind me. I turn in time to see the wide window above the kitchen sink shattering. Water is pouring inside. It doesn't feel real. It looks like a scene out of a movie, when somebody has accidentally broken a large aquarium's glass wall. I expect plastic lobsters and fake fish to start flooding onto the floor. I expect the director to scream, "*Cut.*" I jump to my feet. But it's hard to stay standing. There is a force stronger than gravity trying to pull me down.

"We're sinking!" Wick yells.

"Who builds a ship with a window?" I ask.

Nobody answers me. I find it hard to believe that we're actually going down. I watch Wick and Dale pull Skate to his feet and drag him off the bed and up the stairs.

"Enid, come on!" Wick yells over his shoulder.

I'm surprised that I'm still standing in the water. I thought I was moving. I push my legs through the rising tide. The water is up to my knees, and the boat continues to yank me off balance. I see my shoes floating and pick them up. They're one of my mother's most expensive pairs. I can't leave them. I keep one in my good hand and tuck the other under my arm as I climb the stairs.

When I get on deck, the wind is so powerful that it almost knocks me backward. The rain strikes me so hard that it feels like it could scrape away my skin. The boat lists heavily to one side, and I resist sliding down toward the water. My bare feet squeak against the wet boards as I climb the deck and grab onto the metal railing. I tighten my grip and look over my shoulder at the sinking side of the ship. The sails must be broken. They're flapping in the wind, stiffly cracking with each strong gust. I don't know anything about boats. I don't know if there's something that I should be doing to try to save the ship. There aren't any life jackets in sight. I don't see any life rafts. If I let go of the railing, I'd slide across the deck and fall into the ocean. What would happen to me then?

I turn my head and try to look for Landon, but I don't see him. I don't see Burr either.

"Enid, we need to jump off!" Wick yells.

He's standing by my side, but I didn't even realize it. Skate is next to him. He's standing on his own, but he seems unsteady. I don't know how long he'll be able to swim.

"Wait!" I cry. "I forgot my keys. How will I get back to Vermont?" Like an idiot, I turn to go get them from the bathroom.

Wick grabs my arms. "I think they're gone."

I tug against him. He pulls back.

"Enid! You're not getting your keys."

"Right," I say. I'm not thinking straight. I shouldn't be worried about it. My mom must have a spare set. I look to Wick and then back to the water. Why am I still thinking about the keys?

Below me, the sea is roiling itself into endless waves. Some of them crash onto the ship and try to wash me away. I keep spitting. Somehow the salty water insists on finding its way into my mouth.

Wick says something else, but I can't hear him. I'm in shock. Holding the metal railing, looking into the black water, I have the feeling that I'm going to die. I have the feeling that we're all going to die.

Dale jumps into the water first. His head is barely visible above the rolling waves. We all need to jump now, or we'll get separated. I know this. But I'm unable to follow Dale over the side. I want another choice.

"Are you ready?" Wick asks.

I look down at myself. My skirt sticks to my legs. They're so cold that they don't feel like my legs. I reach down and touch my thigh. It doesn't feel real. None of this feels real.

Wick yells to Dale to get ready, that Skate is coming in next. The wind churns the sea, and this sound along with the wind itself absorbs all the noise around me.

I see Skate's body and blond head bump against the ship as he falls into the ocean. It looked like a painful drop. That is not the way I should fall. When I go in, I need to push off from the boat. On the ship's side I can see the word *Gretchen* written in loopy cursive letters. *Why couldn't she have been a stripper?* And now I'm crying again, like this boat is a real person. She is going to sink to the bottom of the ocean and stay there forever. After all the time it took to make her. After all the money it took to buy her. She'll rot. Disintegrate. She'll be nothing. This is so sad. I may never stop crying. It must be part of witnessing a disaster. You're full of all these feelings, and none of them make total sense.

Before Wick jumps, he grabs my hand. "We should go together," he screams. "Let go of your shoes."

I shake my head.

"Enid, stop thinking like a girl. You don't need your shoes."

Rain drips off his chin and spills down his chest. I want to disagree with him. I don't know that I'm thinking like a girl. I'm thinking like a considerate borrower. The shoes aren't mine to leave. Before I can say this, my feet slip. I almost slide into the water.

"Drop them!"

I let one fall, but I keep the other one tucked under my arm. Wick doesn't notice. I let Wick take my hand. My body must be full of adrenaline. Wick's firmly holding the hand I cut, but it doesn't hurt. It actually feels good. His fingers wrap around mine, and his touch is solid and strong. He jumps first and tugs me in after him. But when we hit the water, we split apart. At first, I panic. I swing my arms out, trying to find him. But a wave crashes over my head, and my open mouth takes in water. I can't panic. I need to swim. I know how to swim. I can do this.

Enid, you're a fish, I tell myself. I roll onto my stomach and extend my arms and legs. The water feels warmer than the air. It feels good to be in the water. The waves are powerful, and I have to learn to ride with them. But I can do this. My main concern is to get away from the ship. I don't want it to pull me down when it sinks. And I think I can feel it. I think I can feel the ship sucking the ocean down around it. With my head down, I take long strokes. I'm moving in the direction that I last saw Wick. I keep going. I don't look up.

I'm worried about Sov and Munny. For some reason,

they both flicker through my mind. They're not strong swimmers. I saw them once in the pool. They weren't exactly flailing, but they didn't have any fluidity about their movements. They will not be able to swim under these conditions. I kick harder. Does this mean they're going to die? That just like *Gretchen*, they'll sink to the bottom of the Atlantic Ocean and rot? I continue to unleash powerful kicks. I need to feel like I'm making progress. Now is not the time to think about Sov and Munny or what I'll tell their bereaved parents.

Where's my brother? I need to find Landon. And Wick. I strain to keep my head high enough above water. The tall waves lift me up. I must be climbing an entire story. Then they flatten. I feel fragile. The sea picks me up and drops me down. I search the curling ocean for Landon and Wick. I don't see anybody. The possibility that I'm alone fills me with terror. I swim back the way I came. The water continues to pick me up. The waves crest with deafening noise. It is so dark. The sea is so big.

As I return to the sinking ship, I see something yellow bobbing in the water. I know that it must be a person. I think of Sov and his yellow shirt. It must be him. He's not dead. I'm not alone. I can do this. I take a deep breath and push through the rough water, trying to reach that yellow mark, as something like happiness comes over me.

chapter 9

One of the first and most vivid memories I have in life is being surrounded by water when I was six. My father and I were seated on a giant plastic swan in a pond at an amusement park.

At the last minute, Landon had refused to board his swan. He felt that it looked like a sissy. "I want to ride a boy bird," he said.

"That one is a boy bird," my mother said.

But Landon wouldn't get on the swan.

"It looks like it's about to lay an egg," he said. "Boys don't do that."

My mother stayed with him. My father was amused. I wasn't concerned about any potential egg-laying issues. I felt perfectly safe. He held my hand as we pedaled with our feet and circled the pond. At first, I liked it. I was on top of the water. I could reach in and touch it with my hand, drawing my fingers across its surface. But our swan was broken. We were supposed to be able to steer it by using a knob in the center console. On our first attempt to turn, it broke off in my father's hand.

Our swan's rudder was stuck, and we pulled to the right. We began to drift past the roped-off area. Fear overwhelmed me. I didn't know how to swim. On the dock, I could see my mother and Landon waving. They thought we were fooling around. They didn't understand that we couldn't get back to them. Our swan continued to drift.

Eventually, we approached a large stone wall. I closed my eyes. The plastic beak rubbed against the rock-hard surface. When I finally looked, there was a long black scuff mark. Beneath its black paint, our swan's beak was a dull pink. The scraped patch resembled a wound. I was sure it was the end for us and the swan. I remember thinking that, like stones, we were all going to sink to the bottom of the pond. Would I ever see Landon or my mother again? No. I folded my hands in my lap. The water now felt dangerous.

My father kept telling me not to cry, that we would be okay, that he wasn't going to let anything bad happen to me. He said that we would look back at this and laugh.

Finally, a man with a long hook arrived. He stood on the sidewalk that wrapped around the pond and leaned over to reach us. He caught our swan by its neck and dragged us back to the landing area. Once it was over, the man with the hook gave me a hug and a coupon for a snow cone. I chose a cherry one, and after I ate it, I threw it up. On the way home, I threw up again, in a paper bag in the backseat. Landon rubbed my back.

"It was trying to get to the grass to lay its eggs," he said.

"No," my mother said. "She just broke."

Landon leaned his mouth to my ear and whispered, "Girl birds are very dangerous."

My mother heard him. "Boy birds are just as dangerous as girl birds," she said sternly.

The following week, my dad enrolled Landon and me in swim classes at the YMCA.

As I move toward the yellow mark several yards in front of me, I think of this swan, and am grateful for it and the swim lessons. The yellow something isn't Sov's shirt. It's a life jacket. Two people are holding each other. One is wearing the jacket. It's Munny and Sov. They see me and yell for me to come.

"Where's Landon?" I ask. Waves splash over my face. My eyes burn from the salt and wind.

"Getting the boat," Sov yells.

I turn and look at *Gretchen*. Only the top of her mast is visible, and it's going down fast. Soon there is nothing but floating debris.

"The boat's gone," I say. "What do you mean?"

"The lifeboat is floating away. He's trying to save it."

The idea that there might be a lifeboat to climb into relieves me. Landon is a strong swimmer. Things are looking up. Again I try to lift my head high enough out of the water to see.

"What about Burr?" I ask.

"He went belowdecks to call the Coast Guard," Sov hollers. "We never saw him come back up."

This doesn't make sense to me. I was belowdecks with Wick, Dale, and Skate when the ship began to sink. I know

Burr wasn't there. I continue to tread water and stay close to Sov and Munny. I'm glad they have a life jacket, even if they have to share it. I'm not sure they could stay afloat without it.

"Where's Wick?" Munny asks. "And Skate and Dale?"

I point in the direction of where I last saw them. To my amazement, I see three figures, and one of them has a bright white mop of hair.

"They're there!" I yell. "They're right there!"

Sov and Munny nod. We all start screaming for them to join us. Slowly, they drift our way. Dale arrives first.

"Where's Burr and Landon?" He's spitting out seawater and his eyes look scared.

I shake my head. I don't know where they are. Wick swims toward us. Skate is with him. Skate doesn't look totally here.

"Help him," I yell to Dale.

Dale reaches out and pulls Skate toward him. He holds him with one arm, helping him stay afloat.

I turn my head back to Sov and Munny.

"What direction did Landon go?" I ask.

Munny is shivering. He raises his arm and yells, "That's him!"

I follow Munny's hand. Many, many yards away I see a person. Whoever it is has a hold of an overturned rubber raft. I set off toward him. My limbs are heavy. I thought catastrophes were supposed to make people feel superhuman. Like they can lift cars off babies. That's not what my body feels like at all. I could use a nap. And a lot of Diet Coke. Maybe some pizza.

I get close enough to the raft to see that it's Landon. But he's not looking at me. He's looking at the spot where *Gretchen* went down. There's nothing there now but ocean. I swim to him and touch his arm. When he looks at me, his eyes become very sad. He shakes his head.

"Oh God, am I dead?" he asks. He starts to cry and slap the water. "I don't feel like I'm dead," he shouts. "I feel like I'm still trying."

It takes me a second to understand why Landon is saying these things. He never knew I was on the boat. He doesn't understand why I'm here.

"You're not dead," I scream. I hook my left arm onto the raft, and with my right hand I gently touch his face. "I drove down from Vermont. I snuck onto the boat. I sank too."

His eyes still look very sad.

"It's bad," he says. "This storm."

"But you saved the raft!"

He shakes his head.

"No. It's just the empty dinghy. The raft with provisions and a beacon blew away. This is nothing."

I try to hug him with one arm.

"It's something," I say. "Let's flip it over and get inside."

He shakes his head again. His teeth are chattering.

"It'll blow away. The wind will catch her and send her off like a kite. That's what happened to the other raft. I'm lucky I snagged this at all."

"Let's try," I say. I want to get out of the water.

I'm tired of treading to stay afloat.

"No, Enid. It's a bad idea. We'll try it after the storm."

I keep holding on to the raft. It's fully inflated, and there's no give in its plastic sides. It would be easier if my hands were bigger. To secure a firm grip, I feel like I'm trying to palm a basketball. It's almost easier not to hold on. I let go.

"Hold the rope," Landon yells. "You need to save your energy."

"The rope?" I reach for it and dangle from the raft. We kick toward the others.

"Skate is hurt," I say.

Landon nods.

"He fell," I yell. I don't tell Landon that I think it was my fault.

"Don't talk. Just kick," he says.

I do as he says. He thinks that we have to wait to turn the raft over. He thinks that the storm will end. When I look around at the wild waves, I find it hard to imagine that this will ever end. The waves and wind feel strong enough to last forever. Dale swims over and grabs hold of the raft too. He also suggests turning it over. Landon explains why we can't. Dale isn't happy.

"Who died and made you captain?" Dale shouts.

"Burr!" Landon says.

I feel sick. I can't believe what Landon has said. Burr can't be dead. He's somewhere. We just have to find him. Sov and Munny meet up with us and attach themselves to the raft. They are smiling. It's a weird picture to see them sopping wet, clinging to each other in the middle of the Atlantic. They don't belong in this disaster. They are two people I always expect to see safe and dry.

Landon lets go of the raft and swims to Wick. Together they pull Skate over. He seems a little better. Once they get him here, he's able to hold on by himself. He's looking around for Burr. He closes his eyes, then asks, "Where is he?"

"We don't know," Landon yells.

Skate leans his head against the side of the raft. He's crying. "It's my fault," he says. "I'm the one who wanted to go out on the water."

He starts to cry harder, and I look away. I turn my focus to the sea. I don't believe that Burr is dead. I believe that he's out there somewhere. If I look hard enough, I'm sure that I can find him.

My body shivers and I can't make it stop. It's kicked into survival mode. I know from a weekend survival class for an overnight snow trip that I took my freshman year that when a body drops below its core temperature, it will shiver in an attempt to warm itself again. The average body, if it's healthy, runs a temperature of 98.6 degrees. Our class instructor was a retired firefighter named Mr. Husky. I can hear his exact words.

If your temperature drops to ninety to ninety-five degrees, it's considered mildly hypothermic. Dropping to eighty-six to ninety degrees is moderately hypothermic. Less than eighty-six degrees is severely hypothermic. It's potentially fatal. Wet conditions are the most dangerous. Get to a dry place immediately and remove wet clothes. Now I almost laugh at that suggestion. I don't imagine that stripping down to a totally nude state will improve our cause. Instead of a wilderness survival class, I wish I had signed up for ocean safety.

Sov and Munny have just finished yelling for Burr. It's my turn. "Burr! Burr!" I don't recognize my voice. It's the most desperate sound I've ever heard. "Burr!" I won't stop screaming because I know he's out there. I yell his name over and over. Nothing happens. I hear Sov and Munny yelling again. My voice grows so thin, I stop. After a few more tries, they stop.

I am so close to Sov and Munny I can hear their teeth chattering. They are the thinnest of all of us. They lack muscle and precious body fat. I'm the next thinnest. I think of all the cake and pies and cookies and marzipan I never ate. I wish I had devoured them. Being a size six here is of no use to me. I wish I weighed twenty pounds more. I wish my thighs were more squatty. In addition to being warmer, I'd also be more buoyant.

"I can't scream anymore," I tell Landon.

"It's okay," he says. He screams a few times, but stops.

"We'll drift together?" I ask. "Right? Once the storm dies down we can find him then?"

Landon looks surprised by my question. "I don't know where he'll end up."

When is Landon going to learn that sometimes in life it's better to lie?

"I'm so cold," I tell him. He nods. It's not just the water, it's the wind. I think about telling him that, but I'm so cold that it's actually difficult for my mouth to form words. We've been in the water less than an hour. I need to stop complaining, because there is nothing anyone can do.

I turn around and look at Sov and Munny.

"Have you decided to stop yelling for Burr?" I ask. I sound like I'm accusing them of something. I'm not.

"We'll try again later," Munny says.

I don't like hearing this, but I don't start screaming again either.

We've arranged ourselves around the raft so that we make a balanced circle. I can't see Wick, Dale, or Skate. They're all on the other side. I get ready to turn back around and face Landon again, when I feel a warm patch of water float past me. It feels good. I wish there was more of it.

"I'm sorry," Sov yells.

I don't understand what he's apologizing for.

"I peed," he says. He looks right at me, mildly ashamed. "Fact of life."

That warm water was urine? Great. I can't believe that I think this, but I actually wish it would happen again. The ocean is robbing my body of heat. As I kick and struggle to stay afloat, my body tries to warm itself, but the sea won't let it.

At one point, a large wave comes and knocks me under the raft. I panic. I think that I'm going to drown. Then I realize that beneath the raft is a pocket of calm air. There's no light. It has an eerie and cavelike feel, but it's completely out of the storm. Landon pops his head in to make sure that I'm all right.

"We should come under the raft," I say. I don't have to yell to be heard. Within these plastic walls, there's no wind. "We should get out of the wind."

"Good idea," he says.

I exit the shelter and pull myself back into the storm. I need to convince Sov and Munny to go under the raft. They understand exactly what I'm saying, and they lower themselves enough to slip under the raft's side. Landon has gone to the other side of the raft to explain this idea to the rest of the guys. Even though I want the calm, it's hard for me to go. Because then I'm not going to be able to look for Burr. I'll have to admit that he's really gone.

I shout one last time for him.

"Burr," I scream. "Are you out there?"

Again I look into the rolling and crashing waves. I don't see Burr, but I think I hear him. He's howling. Nobody else is around. I need to tell someone. Then I worry that I may be wrong. In the weekend survival course, Mr. Husky also said that as hypothermia sets in, the mind starts to unwind. Slowly, you go crazy and you don't even realize it. What does it matter? I need to try. I don't want to be the kind of person who's only concerned with saving herself.

I'm a strong swimmer. I should try to look for him. Wouldn't I want somebody to look for me? Just as I'm about to go under the raft, I push out into the darkness, instead. It feels like I'm swimming into an abyss. I kick further into the black water. After a few strokes I stop. "Burr! Burr!" I think of what my mother said. *They're like our own family.* I scream for him again. I yell so loudly that it feels like my throat and lungs could burst. I stop. I spit out seawater. I want to find him. But the waves are too big. I can't do this. I turn to swim back.

Skate is swimming toward me. This makes no sense. He's hurt. He should have stayed with the raft. "Go back!" I yell.

He looks at me the same way Landon looked at me.

Skate is scared to his soul. He even asks the same question.

"Am I dead?"

I shake my head. It's the second time tonight I've been mistaken for some sort of grim reaper.

"I was on the boat, too, remember?" I explain. "I was in the bathroom."

He looks confused. That's when I begin to understand what's really happening. My mind is mixing things up. This is Burr! I try to explain things better.

"I came to talk to Wick," I say. "The raft is this way!"

"Thank God," he says.

He swims after me, and I hope I'm not wrong. What if I'm turned around? What if they drifted away?

I wasn't wrong. I see the raft, but because everybody is under it, it looks abandoned.

Burr grabs on to the side of it.

"Are you okay?" I ask. Which, as soon as I say it, seems like a stupid question. None of us is *okay*.

"My head hurts, but I'm fine," he yells. "I can't believe I found you."

I don't let this pass. "I found you!" It matters to me that he understands that this wasn't a coincidence. I want him to know that I was risking my life out there.

I can smell the beer on his breath, but I don't think that he's totally drunk.

"We're all here," I say.

He looks at me in disbelief. I guess that makes sense, because he can't see anybody but me.

"Where's Skate?" he asks.

"We're under the raft."

I try to show him with my hand that we need to dive under the side. He nods. When both of our heads resurface in the calm pocket, I say, "I found Burr!"

"Burr!" Skate says. I feel Burr swim away from me toward the other end of the raft. Inside this pocket it's impossible to see anything.

"Are you okay?" Burr asks.

"Yeah," Skate says. "You?"

"I'm good."

Everyone is speaking. We're in an echo chamber. I focus on keeping my head at a perfect level so that I don't swallow any more water. We take turns saying things like, "We are so lucky." Things now feel like they're going to turn out okay. I mean, isn't that how some disasters end? Everybody walks away from the ordeal with wounds that will eventually heal? And then we write gut-wrenching, inspirational books about it? While at the same time we pursue amazingly demanding professions? And we're so thrilled with our jobs and our families and our lives that we eagerly wake up every day and kiss everybody we love on the forehead? It feels like an option. At this point, a happy ending seems totally within our reach.

"How are you feeling?" Landon asks.

"Are you asking me?" I say.

"Skate," Landon says.

"I'm okay," Skate say.

But I know that's not the truth. Burr should know. Somebody should tell Burr that Skate hurt his head. I'd want to know if Landon was injured. We shouldn't be lying to each other about our physical conditions. There are rules to lying. It's okay to lie to make people feel better. But you should never lie if it endangers somebody's life. We should be totally honest. We need to depend on each other. I decide I should tell Burr.

"Skate isn't okay," I say. "He hit his head."

"I'm fine," Skate says. "We don't need drama, Enid."

I can't believe he said that. I kick to stay afloat and unleash more truth.

"He fell coming down the stairs. He slipped. He hurt his head. And he hit the side of the boat jumping off. He's injured."

"Is it bad?" Burr asks.

"It's not bad," Skate says. "Drop it."

"He's good," Wick says.

Wick shouldn't say that. He doesn't know for sure.

Large waves continue to lift up the raft and set her back down. We manage to stay beneath her, treading water. It feels like it's getting darker, even though that's not possible.

"Do you think we'll get rescued tonight?" Munny asks.

"Dude, nobody knows we're out here," Dale says.

"That's not true," Munny says. "Burr called the Coast Guard. They know our ship sank. They're going to come and save us."

I think back to the breaking window. I don't remember Burr ever coming down those stairs.

"You called the Coast Guard?" I ask.

"I did," Burr says. "I gave them our position too. Once the wind dies down, they'll come for us. First with a copter, then I bet they send a cutter."

There is a happy slapping sound. I imagine that it's Landon slapping Burr on the back.

"Good job, man," Landon says. "You're one helluva captain."

We continue to bob. I can feel the presence of the bodies next to me. Even though they are frightened and cold, they seem to be giving off hope. I don't voice my doubt. I too want to believe that the Coast Guard will be coming for us.

chapter 11

I don't know how long we've been under the raft. It's beginning to feel like a rubber cage. And eight animals, let alone teenagers, should never be forced to live indefinitely in a rubber cage together.

"The air is too thick in here," Wick says. "We need more oxygen."

He's right. The air beneath the raft is stale, and it's difficult to breathe.

"Let's lift up the raft," Dale says.

"It'll blow away," Landon says.

"We've got to do something," Wick says.

"I say we lift it up," Burr offers.

"That's a bad idea," Landon says. His voice is loud and certain.

I feel like I should agree with Landon, not only because he's my brother, but because he's historically proven himself to be a reasonable person under duress. "I agree with Landon," I say.

"No. We need to lift it," Dale says. "We could die under here."

Nobody wants to die. Nobody wants to hear anybody talking that way.

"We should try it," Wick says.

"I agree," Burr says.

"Yeah," Munny says.

Landon loses out, even with my vote. The guys decide to lift up the right side of the raft. As soon as they do, a gust of wind catches it, and just as Landon warned, flings it out of our grasp. The rubber cage flies across the water. A gust of wind hits my face. As I try to tread water, I instantly am overtaken with feelings of panic and despair.

"Shit," Burr yells.

Burr, Landon, and Wick all start swimming after the flyaway raft. The wind continues to beat against my face. I reach out to Sov and Munny so that we don't drift apart. Waves march over us.

"Dude, it's gone," Dale says.

"No it's not," I say, spitting out water. "You're not even trying."

"Neither are you," he says.

I know he's right, and I shut my mouth. But I'm too tired to swim after it. Sov puts his hand on my shoulder.

"It's okay, Enid," he says. "Do you want to borrow the life jacket?"

"No," I say. "You keep it."

The yellow-and-black jacket is almost too big for Sov. His head could actually fit through one of the armholes. But I think he's wearing it correctly. It's so sweet of Sov to offer it to me. Without it, who knows if he and Munny stand a chance.

I turn and look at Skate, who's able to tread water. He's quiet and not acting like himself. I'm not sure when it happened, but the bandage has slipped off, and I don't see it anywhere. It's too dark to see the wound. After he fell, I was so busy trying to fix the gash that I didn't think about how bad it was. But the cut was so deep, I could see his skull.

When Landon finally reaches the raft, they are close enough that I think I can see that the raft is upside down again. Wick and Burr reach it too, and the three of them begin swimming back to us. When they get here, we all slip under it again, glad to be sheltered from the wind. Living in a rubber cage does have its advantages.

"We all shouldn't come in at the same time," Dale says. "We should take turns. The air will turn to crap again."

"We're not sending anyone out into the storm," Landon says.

I'm not used to seeing him be so assertive. But I'm relieved, because I think that he's absolutely right.

"We need good air or we'll suffocate," Dale says. "We'll die."

The word *die* hangs in the air. Dale really needs to quit saying that word.

"I have an idea," Munny says. "Next time the air gets thick, we can lift up the raft on the side that isn't opposite the wind. If we do it carefully, just a little, the raft won't blow away."

His suggestion is followed by silence.

"Good idea," Skate says.

These are the first words that Skate has spoken in a very long time.

"I think that will work," Burr adds.

"If we're careful," Landon says.

"I don't think that will work," Dale says. "We need to take turns. What if one of us suffocates? It's so dark under here, we wouldn't even know anybody had died." His voice is thunderous beneath the raft.

There's a splash. Then another. Wick has grabbed Dale by his shirt and shoved him. Wick pulls Dale close to his face.

"Stop saying we're gonna die," Wick says. "I mean it." Dale pushes Wick away.

"Don't fight," I say. "I think it uses more oxygen."

"We should take turns. Pick numbers," Dale says. "There isn't enough oxygen under here for eight people."

"We're not picking numbers," Landon says. He's moved closer to Wick and Dale. "Stay over here, Enid."

I feel like Dale's comment was directed at me. Because I wasn't supposed to be here. I am taking up oxygen. "You're making me feel guilty for being alive," I say.

"We need more air," Dale says.

I feel a hand on my shoulder. My whole body tightens. Then I realize it's Burr.

"Enid, don't feel guilty. God, you helped me find you guys. Without you, I never would have spotted you or the raft."

This response brings silence. I'm glad Burr stuck up for me. But I can't quite shake this sudden onset of guilt. "Thanks," I say. "But I really shouldn't be here." I say that last sentence in a whisper. I try to take fewer breaths.

Landon moves to my side and brushes up against me.

"The Coast Guard will find us soon. We can talk about that later."

I keep treading water.

"I'm so cold," I say.

"We all are," Landon says.

"Let's huddle together," I suggest.

"I can't believe this has happened. I'm so pissed," Dale says. He swats at the water and makes a slash.

"Get over it," Burr says. "Enid's right. We should huddle."

We move together and pack ourselves into a tight circle. It helps a little. We all tread water. The waves have calmed. The sea continues to pick us up and set us down, but it's nothing like those earlier swells. We continue to float beneath the raft. Every hour or so, we gently lift up one side of the raft like Munny suggested. It works. We're able to replenish the air without losing the raft.

"How much longer before the Coast Guard comes?" Wick asks. "Do you really think they'll be able to find us? We've probably drifted pretty far from where the boat went down."

"They're experts," Burr says. "They've got years of experience studying drift patterns. They've got our coordinates. They'll be here before dawn."

It feels good to believe this, so I do.

"When did you call the Coast Guard?" Wick asks.

"Right as she was going down," Burr says. "I barely made it out."

"Man, that's brave," Landon says.

Nobody says anything for a long time. I think we're all stuck on the same thought. We want dawn to come. We want to board a ship again. We're ready for the Coast Guard. We're ready to be safe and dry and home.

chapter 12

Dawn comes and there is no Coast Guard. The first glow of daylight illuminates the world through the raft. I can see everybody. We're all here. I count our heads. Seven. I count my own head. I reach up and touch it and say the word "Eight."

"What are you doing?" Landon asks.

"Counting heads. I'm eight," I say.

"Okay," he says. "Let's get out from under here. It looks like a clear day."

He sounds happy. Nobody has sounded that way for hours.

I lower my head into the water and surface beside the raft. Daylight touches my face, and it feels warm and hopeful. I want to close the distance, to lift myself out of the water and feel baked by the sun until I'm dry. The storm has passed. Not quite flat, the water is calmer now, absent the never-ending, towering waves.

Munny and Sov are beside me. When I look at them they smile. Reflexively, I smile back.

"We made it," Dale says. His voice sounds surprised.

"Maybe we should try to flip the raft over," Skate says.

I turn toward him and see the back of his head. The wound looks worse than I remembered. It's a thick red line nestled between two white folds of skin. I want to ask him if he's feeling okay, but I don't.

"Good idea," Landon says.

Skate's voice seems to be carrying power. Maybe it's because he's the wounded one.

"I think that could work," Landon says. "Let's everybody get on one side."

In unison, Wick, Dale, Landon, and Burr punch at one side of the raft. They coax it with their arms fully outstretched, using the tips of their fingers, until it tumbles over, slapping the ocean's surface. Once it's flipped, the guys turn to me, but I wave them off.

"Munny and Sov first," I say. I'm the best swimmer here. I don't need to go in first.

The guys help Munny and Sov into the raft first. They push them by their butts over the raft's lip. When they land they squeak across the raft's bottom toward an edge.

"You next," Burr says to Skate.

Skate swings his arms into the raft and tries to pull himself up, but he can't. He throws one leg up, and hooks it on the side of the raft. But he doesn't have the strength to pull himself inside. Munny and Sov tug at him. Finally, the guys push him and he rolls into the raft.

"Shit," Skate says. "It's cold."

"It's the wind," Sov says. He's sitting on one of the raft's inflated yellow walls, the wind carrying pieces of his dark hair over his eyes.

"You next," Landon says.

He lifts me halfway up, and I yell for him to drop me.

"What?" he asks. "What is it?"

"It's warmer in the water," I say. The wind is so cold it feels like it's biting me.

"Once you get dry, it will feel warmer," Wick says.

Dale pulls himself up into the raft without any problem.

"You shouldn't stay in the water," Landon says.

"It shows a lack of survival instinct," Dale says.

What a jerk. His comment makes me want to prove him wrong and stay in the water even longer. "I'm fine," I say.

Everyone sits inside the raft, spaced around the perimeter to help balance the vessel. It needs to stay balanced so it can ride out the small waves. The sun is visible for the first time in a long time behind puffs of gray clouds. I have my arm draped over the side and Wick is holding my hand. I don't know why I feel so optimistic, but I'm certain that any minute I'm going to see the Coast Guard, that they're going to take me home.

"Nobody is going to believe this," Dale says. "We're going to be able to sell this story."

"Sort of depends on how it ends," Munny said.

"I know how it will end," Burr says.

My left arm feels tired. It starts to cramp. I let go of Wick's hand. I switch so I'm holding the raft with my other arm.

"How's that?" I ask. Not only am I curious, I want the distraction. Burr doesn't answer me. Not being inside the raft makes me feel more extraneous than ever. I want to feel like I'm part of the group. My mind zooms to the e-zine again. I should not be thinking about that. It's petty. I ask my question louder. "How's that?"

Burr peers over the raft's side so he can look directly at me. This gesture makes me (and my question) feel relevant, and I like that. "We're still going to bob for a couple more hours. At some point we'll empty our pockets and find out that one of us salvaged a candy bar. We'll all split that. Then something will happen." Burr doesn't say anything else. The silence bothers me.

"What will happen?" I ask.

"I don't know. We'll all have to face some obstacle. And then one of us will emerge as the big hero. In every survivor story there's always that one guy who does something that everybody says, 'Holy shit. He was the hero.' And then we get saved and end up on television."

There's more silence.

"That sounds good," Wick says.

But I'm still thinking about what that thing is that's going to happen.

"I wonder what kind of candy bar one of us salvaged," Dale says. "Let's empty our pockets now."

"Let's wait," Burr says. "Let's be mellow and hang."

"The sun looks amazing," Skate says.

It hits me that this was the reason they took the boat out to begin with. They wanted to watch dawn from the water.

"Are you okay?" Landon asks.

Nobody answers.

"Me?" I ask. "I'm fine. I'm going to float."

I let my legs lift up and I recline. I stare up into the sky. Water enters my ears, and I can't hear anything. I feel like I'm falling down staircases inside of myself. I close my eyes. I could stay like this for a long time. Hours. I'm hardly using any energy. Maybe by the time I'm tired of floating, a rescue ship will arrive. Maybe it will arrive *before* I get tired of floating. I need to stay positive. I feel a bump from beneath me against my right hip. I open my eyes. I see an arm flying at a frightening speed toward me. It's Wick. He yanks on me hard. But I'm confused. I resist.

"You're hurting me," I say. His hand is gripped firmly around my arm.

"Get out of the water, Enid!"

I let him lift me. My legs still dangle in the ocean.

"Get your legs in the boat!" Wick says. "Now!"

I swing my legs in the raft. Landon's arm has a hold of them, and even once I'm totally in the raft, he doesn't let go of me.

"Jesus," Dale says.

I look into the water. I can't believe what I see. It's a shark. Once I figure out what it is, I can't stop staring at its dorsal fin. I am in shock. I see movement a few feet away. I let my focus widen. As I sit in the raft, shaking, I see at least a dozen fins.

"They're everywhere," Burr says.

"Do you think they're man-eaters?" Landon asks.

I don't say anything, but I totally think they are man-eaters. First, I once attempted to watch Shark Week on the Discovery Channel. Second, why else would they be here?

Did they come to eat the raft? Oh my God. A new fear sweeps over me. Do sharks eat rafts? I replay everything I can remember from the two hours I managed to endure of Shark Week, and then move on to *Jaws*. Didn't the shark in that eat several people? And a dog? And air tanks? And a helicopter?

"I think they might be man-eaters," Burr says. "Sharks in water this deep are opportunistic feeders. They think we're their next opportunity."

If it wanted to, when it bumped me, the shark could have eaten me in a few bites. And right now, instead of listening to Burr, I'd be dead. Dead. Me. Now. The circumstances of my life have become too crazy. I don't want this. Boring as it is, I want my old life. Considering what I have here, I'd prefer an unvarying and tedious life punctuated by moments of ennui and weariness until I become a senior citizen. Then let me die. And let that death be shark-free.

"Are they real?" I hear myself ask.

"*Real?*" Dale says. "We're lucky they didn't bite our asses off last night."

"Your ass? They would have bitten our legs off first," Munny says.

"Most likely," Sov adds.

"Shut up," Burr says. "Let's try to stay positive. This is the thing that happens, and now Wick is the hero."

I look at Wick. He is pale white, and his bottom lip seems to be trembling. "My girlfriend almost got eaten by a shark."

It is ridiculous for my heart to leap at hearing Wick refer to me as his girlfriend. But it does. I'm happy I'm alive. I'm happy he saved me. I am thrilled we're back together.

"What the hell are we supposed to do?" Dale asks.

We all look into the ocean. The fins exist. Some of the sharks are bold enough to bump against the raft with their noses and sides. I find it hard not to hypothesize, at least to myself, about the order in which a shark will eat my body parts.

"Why didn't we see them before?" I ask.

"Sharks like to feed at dawn and dusk," Munny says.

I actually think I can remember that from Shark Week. "What do we do now?"

As I'm speaking, a large wave comes and nearly dumps us into the ocean. I scream. Wick grabs my waist and pulls me on his lap. Sov and Munny lower themselves into the bottom of the raft. Because of where he's sitting, Skate is knocked into the raft's center. The rest of the guys stay seated on the edge, holding tightly to the side. After the raft settles, the water around us foams.

"We need to keep it balanced," Landon says. "We always need to watch for the big waves."

Triangular fins continue to rise and fall in the water, cutting through the sea like the tips of dark knives. I try to tell myself that *Jaws* was just a movie. That I'm safe in the raft. I try to convince myself that they're just curious and will eventually go away. But then I remember something else from Shark Week. A show where sharks tore apart seals and seal-shaped plastic boards. The sharks breached and chomped for two entire hours.

"This is just like *Jaws*," Dale says.

I hate that Dale and I could be thinking nearly the same thought. I want our brains to be running on very different wavelengths.

"That was just a movie," I say.

"Actually, I think it was based on a true story," Wick says.

"You're right," Sov says. "A shark went crazy and started killing swimmers. It even attacked them in rivers."

"Shut up," Burr says. "We can't focus on crap like that."

Skate nods in agreement. "Stay positive."

"Do you think this is what survivors are supposed to be talking about? We're survivors. Now let's focus on staying safe until we're rescued," Burr says.

"I totally don't think of you as the captain anymore," Dale says. "I mean, I sort of blame you."

"I don't care if you blame me. Just knock off the *Jaws* talk."

"I agree," I say. "Let's stop talking about sharks."

Dale points into the ocean at a passing fin.

"I think our situation speaks for itself."

"Don't look in the water," Landon says. "I agree with Burr and Enid. Let's stay positive. Let's focus on staying safe."

I adjust my position in the boat. I just now realized that my skirt is so wet that it's nearly transparent. So is my shirt. When it comes to my private parts, I'm not leaving much to the imagination. I cross my legs and fold my arms across my chest. I look at my bare feet.

"I wish I would've worn something more appropriate," I say.

Landon rolls his eyes.

"I feel a little exposed is all."

"We'll be rescued soon. None of us is really dressed for a nautical disaster," Landon says.

He smiles at me. It almost makes me feel better, and I consider smiling back. But as I survey their clothes, I realize that the guys are all dressed for a nautical disaster far better than I am. Except for Sov and Munny, they're all wearing jeans. And their T-shirts don't look as flimsy as my ridiculous blouse. And Dale is fortunate enough to be wearing a Windbreaker. I've made the worst wardrobe mistake of my life. And I'm haunted by it. I close my eyes and rest my head on the raft's side.

"You really think somebody has a candy bar?" Dale asks.

"What?" I ask.

"I'm talking to Burr. He said that somebody would have a candy bar," Dale says.

"I think if one of us had food, they would have offered it up by now." I am so thirsty my mouth feels unfamiliar.

"I don't have food," Munny says. "But maybe we should empty our pockets and see if any of us have anything useful."

"Good idea," Sov says. "Maybe we have something that can attract food."

"Yeah," Wick says.

I don't have anything in my pockets. Because my skirt was white and formfitting, and I didn't want to create bulges at my hips, I'm not even carrying any ChapStick.

Landon empties his pockets first. There are some coins, wet mushy receipts, and two soggy twenties.

My nagging hunger leads me to ask a stupid question. "Do bills have any nutrients? Can we eat money?"

Munny shakes his head. "It's cloth. And it's saturated in salt."

"The Coast Guard will be here soon. This is just an activity that gives us something to do," Burr says.

"Not for me," Dale says. "I'm hoping we find something that we can use to catch fish."

What could any of the guys have in their pockets that could be used to catch fish?

Munny has some change.

"Don't you guys have any wallets with pocketknives?" I ask.

Dale groans. "Who carries a pocketknife in his wallet? That's retarded."

"We put all our wallets and cell phones in a drawer belowdecks," Wick says. "Burr suggested we do that because once while night sailing, they hit choppy water and his wallet and phone went overboard."

"So you knew you could hit dangerous water and you went out anyway?" I ask.

I'm madder about this than I realize. When it first happened, I thought, well, this is my fault because I drove here. But now I'm thinking, no, this is all their fault because they took the boat out.

"Pockets. Pockets," Wick says. "Let's focus on pockets."

Wick has less than twenty dollars. It's a mix of fives and ones. Sov has quarters and two old movie tickets. Burr has five bucks. Dale has three dollars and a pale pink pebble. He takes it out and then puts it back in his pocket.

"What's that for?" Wick asks.

"It's nothing," Dale says.

"Maybe we can use it," I say. Isn't that the whole point of this exercise?

"You know I have it. If you think of something we can use it for, I'll pull it back out."

He is so difficult. Why can't he be more like his brother? I look around at the random junk pulled from all the guys' pockets. I'm surprised. I thought there would be something valuable besides minimal amounts of cash.

"What can we make with this?" Dale says.

"Wait, let's not give up," Wick says.

I glance back and forth between them. This is a typical way they interact, so typical it reminds me of Dale's reaction to one of our twin tests: the situational-problem-solving exam. We're often given a series of multiple-choice questions meant to measure our problem-solving styles. I tend to forget them as soon as I answer them, but Wick often retains nearly the whole test and drills Dale about his answers on the drive home. Once, a question asked what you'd do if everyone you worked with got a new computer except for you. You were given a few possible reactions to choose from. I don't remember the options. But Wick said he would assume it had been a mistake and ask to see his supervisor. I answered that way too.

But Dale said he'd take a new computer from a coworker. Wick mocked his brother's problem-solving abilities the entire way home. And then, at a stoplight, Dale reached around from the backseat and smacked Wick in the head. Hard. I couldn't believe it. Luckily, Landon was there, and he broke up the fight. I remember thinking that day that Wick and Dale couldn't be more different. I don't even understand how Dale can be related to the rest of his family.

Wick takes a dollar and folds it lengthwise four times. "If we tear these into strips and tie them together we can create a line to dangle in the water. We can fish."

"Couldn't you use your shoelaces?" I ask. That seems simpler.

"No way." Dale says this emphatically. "If we hit an island, we'll need our shoelaces because we'll need our shoes. We might have to outrun a wild animal."

"What?" I ask. I think I must have misheard him.

"What if we end up beached on a deserted island that has wild boars?" Dale says.

"Shouldn't we focus on scenarios that will actually happen?" I ask.

"I agree," Landon says. "The dollars work fine."

Munny shakes his head. "We don't have a hook."

Wick begins to tear the dollar. "If we tie a coin at the

bottom and lure the fish to the surface, we can catch them with our hands."

"Really?" I ask. That seems impossible.

"Why would a coin lure fish to the surface?" Burr asks.

"Fish like shiny things," Wick says. "They're like monkeys." He has finished tearing the first dollar and begins on the second.

"That idea seems impossible," Sov says.

Wick doesn't stop tearing.

"It's probably better than doing nothing," Skate says. "Right?"

"I don't know," Dale says. "We're destroying good cash."

I am so thirsty. My head is pounding. I'm tired. If Wick wants to tear apart all the bills and tie them together and attach loose change to them, then I am going to let him do that. "I'm going to take a nap." I move to the bottom of the raft to sit. Dirty water pools around me, but I don't care. I don't want to risk falling asleep on the raft's side. What if I slipped? What if a shark came? What if, unlike last time, nobody saved me? I wonder what it feels like to die.

I wake up and notice that Skate and Burr are both sleeping. So is Dale. So are Sov and Munny. It's one of the few options we have on the raft. For the first time I take stock of everyone's feet. Sov's and Munny's, like mine, are bare. The rest of the guys are wearing sneakers. I wish I had sneakers. The sun is shining a little stronger now, burning off the clouds. Wick and Landon have tied together all the money, making a long, thin rope of cash.

"Do you really think you'll be able to catch a fish?" I ask. Looking at the fully assembled line, it seems beyond impossible.

"We'll try," Wick says.

They toss it into the water, and the quarter tied to the end drags the line down. I watch it sink. I keep hoping that a big fish will arrive. I'm hungry. I'm really hungry. Wick tugs the quarter to the surface and then it beings to descend again. It mesmerizes me.

"What do you think Mom is doing?" Landon asks. "How do you think the Coast Guard will tell her? Do they call, or send somebody to the door?"

I think back to the last time I saw my mother. She looked so small and anxious. Oh God. I wonder what she did when she found the marzipan bride and groom.

"Enid?" Wick asks. "Did you zone out? Landon asked you a question."

I lick my lips. They are so dry they ache. My tongue is dry too. "I don't know how the Coast Guard notifies families. I'm not sure how they'd know exactly who was on the boat."

I lift myself from the soppy bottom of the raft and sit on a side next to Wick.

"I left her at the Sheraton," I say.

"Who?" Wick asks.

"My mother."

"What did you use as an excuse?" Landon asks.

I shrug. "I didn't make any. I just left. I damaged some marzipan and dropped it off on the sidewalk for her and drove down. I think I snapped."

"Jesus," Landon says. "You abandoned Mom at the Sheraton. That's mean."

He's right. But it didn't seem mean at the time. It seemed necessary.

"You two shouldn't argue about it now. What's done is done," Wick says.

"I don't know what I was thinking," I say. After watching the quarter fall for the umpteenth time, I decide I'd like to be in charge of it for a while. "Can I drop the coin?"

"You can't drop it," Landon says. "You just let it fall a little, and then you pull it back up."

"That's what I meant," I say.

"Sure," Landon says.

Wick moves over so I can pass him to get to where Landon is, and when he docs that, he bumps Dale awake.

"It is so frigging hot," Dale says. "I hope it rains."

I sit next to Landon. "I don't. Think of the waves. I'd rather have calm seas and warm temperatures."

"Rain doesn't have to mean storm," Dale says.

At the sound of the word storm, Burr stirs and wakes up. "Next time I wake up, I'm hoping to see a rescue ship."

"That would be nice," I say.

"I'm so hungry. Does anyone have any food?" Dale asks.

"I don't," I say. I watch Munny and Sov blink their eyes open.

"Nobody has anything in their pockets?" Dale says.

"I don't have anything," Landon says.

"Me either," Munny says, yawning.

"Nothing," Burr says.

"We've already emptied our pockets," Sov says.

Skate is asleep.

"Did Skate empty his pockets?" Dale asks Burr. "He's been a little out of it. Maybe he forgot to check."

"He doesn't have anything," Burr says. "None of us has anything."

"No Milk Duds, no Junior Mints, no red licorice ropes?" Dale says.

"We were headed sailing," Wick says. "Not to an afternoon matinee."

"I just can't believe that nobody grabbed any chips. We had, like, eight bags of Doritos."

"Good point, Dale. Right as the ship was going under, I asked myself, do I call the Coast Guard? Or secure a couple of bags of Doritos?" Burr says.

"It's great that the Coast Guard is coming, but it would be nice if we had something to eat," Dale says.

Burr looks away and doesn't say anything.

"It's really surprising," Dale says, dangling his hand in the water. "I thought that stuff would float. Shouldn't it be everywhere?"

"It probably floated away," Sov says.

"Maybe your life jacket has something in its pockets? Did you check those?" Dale asks.

Sov shakes his head.

"Nobody has anything. Not even a toothpick. Do you want us to take our pants off so you can check the pockets yourself?" Landon asks.

There's a pause.

"I'm not taking my pants off," Landon says.

"I didn't want you to."

"We're all hungry," Wick says.

I rest my head on Wick's shoulder. I haven't eaten a real meal in over twenty-four hours. Wick cradles me under one arm. As I relax, I'm reminded again how thirsty I am. I lick my lips.

"How long can a person go without water?" I ask.

Actually, I thought I was just thinking the question. I'm surprised when I hear my own voice asking it.

"It depends on the conditions," Munny says.

"I think we know the conditions," Dale says. "These are them."

I glare at Dale.

"I think what Dale was trying to say was that maybe we need to take a status check," Wick says.

"Really?" I ask. We all know our situation is bad.

"Munny, why don't you hit some high points on things we should be thinking about?" Wick says.

"Okay. To avoid getting jungle foot, everyone wearing sneakers should consider taking off your shoes," Munny says.

"I'm not gonna throw my shoes overboard," Dale says.

"Right," I said. "The boar island."

"Shh," Landon says.

"You don't have to throw them over," Munny says. "But think about taking them off."

Dale kicks at the water in the bottom of the raft. "Maybe later," he says.

"Yeah," Burr says. "They feel pretty good now."

"What else?" Landon asks.

"People who drank alcohol will feel the effects of dehydration first," Munny says.

"What?" Dale says. "Are you putting a moral spin on this because you didn't drink anything?" Dale's pink face is creased by lines of anger, especially around his mouth and eyes.

"Those are the facts," Munny says.

"He's telling the truth," Wick says. "I remember this from AP Bio."

I don't know who has been drinking and who hasn't. I mean, I know Burr and Skate were, and I know Sov and Munny weren't, but I don't know about Wick, Dale, or Landon. I'm afraid to bring it up. I guess I don't want the answer.

"The people who were drinking are going to be peeing more than the rest of us. Ethanol depresses the level of arginine vasopressin, or AVP. It's an antidiuretic hormone. This means you'll lose more fluid."

"What?" Dale asks again. His voice sounds alarmed. "What should we do?"

"You should consider drinking your urine," Munny says.

"Holy shit," Dale says. "There's no way I'm drinking my own pee."

"He's right," Wick says. "We should start thinking about stuff like this. It's better than losing all that fluid."

"I've never heard of doing that," Dale says. He looks down at his crotch.

I am tempted to tell him that had he pushed himself and taken AP Bio, maybe he would have heard of doing things like that.

"The Coast Guard will get here before it comes to that," Burr says.

"Enid!" Wick yells.

I flop reflexively into the center of the boat, certain the reason Wick screamed was due to sharks.

"You dropped it," Wick says.

"Enid, if you were tired of holding it you could have given it to me," Landon says.

I don't know what they're talking about.

"Enid, the dollar rope and the quarter," Wick says. "It's halfway down to the bottom of the ocean."

I remember. How could I forget I was holding it? I didn't mean to drop it. I don't feel terrible, because I don't think there's any way we could have really caught a fish by using that method, but I say, "I'm sorry."

"You don't look upset at all," Landon says.

I glance at Landon. The skin below his eyes is a dull gray color. That's what happens when he doesn't get enough sleep.

"I do feel bad. I zoned out. I think I'm still zoning."

Landon looks at me sternly. It isn't until I mouth the words *I'm sorry* that his face softens and he gives me a nod, letting me know I'm forgiven.

"Do you have any extra dollars?" I ask.

"We still have two twenties," Wick says. "I'll see if I can make another line."

"Good," I say.

I sit back and look into the water. It is so never-ending. The sun's glare bounces off the waves, creating a painful halo. If I were a painter or a photographer, maybe I'd think this image was beautiful. Or maybe I would see it as a metaphor for death.

"Okay!" Dale says. "Here's where I stand on drinking my own pee." His voice sounds flat and definitive. "If the Coast Guard doesn't come in three hours, I'll do it. And if Munny and Wick say it's what we should do, we should all do it. And once we get home we never tell anyone. I swear to God. This can't get out. We'll do the things we need to do to survive. We'll act like cave people. Go primal, but when we get home, none of this happened."

I agree with him in a weird way, but I also can't help myself from laughing. Only Dale would get this worked up about the potential rumors involved with drinking urine.

"I have two questions," Burr says.

"Shoot," Dale says.

"How will you know when three hours has passed? And what are you going to use for a cup?" Burr laughs when he's finished. But Dale doesn't.

"Shut up, man. None of this is funny."

"Some of it is," Skate says.

I didn't realize he was awake. I wonder how his head is doing. I wonder if we should dip the wound in the sea to clean it. I close my eyes. Is salt water sterile? Munny would know. Or maybe Wick. I don't think it is.

We drift in silence. Now my mouth feels like it's filled with cotton. My tongue is swollen. The sea looks endless, and I'm reminded of "The Rime of the Ancient Mariner," a Coleridge poem that I wrote a paper on last spring. "Water, water, everywhere, And all the boards did shrink; Water, water, everywhere, Nor any drop to drink." Ms. Fleck loved that paper. I focused on the albatross as a symbol of innocence and femininity. I got an A+, and she asked me to read part of it to the class. But the class hadn't been nearly as moved by my observations of the albatross as Ms. Fleck.

When I go to college, maybe I should study literature and not biology. Maybe I should study both and have a double major. Bio is something I like because Wick and I do it together. But literature has always been something I love. A wave knocks against the raft and brings me back to the moment. I hate the sea for being so salty and ill-tempered. What did I ever do to harm it? I mean, I recycle and everything. I can't take looking at the sharks or the empty horizon. I close my eyes and wonder, how bad is this, *really*?

"This has happened before, right?" I ask. "We can't be the first people whose boat sank."

I think of how easy it was for the window to break and the ship to go down. It happened fast. A lot of waves hit her, and boom, the *Gretchen* was sinking. This has to be somewhat common. There are so many boats in the world. During big storms, a certain percentage must always sink. Maybe this is as common as blowing out a tire.

"Well, there's the *Titanic*," Wick says.

I think he's trying to make me laugh, but it has the opposite effect. His comment makes me feel a little doomed.

"Don't!" Skate says.

I jerk my head to look at him. Burr is touching Skate's wound.

"We need to clean it," Burr says.

I was going to mention that. I feel bad that I forgot to say something.

"We don't have anything," Landon says.

"It's fine," Skate says.

"It's not fine," Burr says. He's parting Skate's blond hair, staring deep into the gash. "There's pus. It's infected. We need to do something."

"Could we clean it with salt water?" I ask.

"We could," Munny says. "But there's bacteria in that too."

"You should dress it," Sov says.

"What about a dress?" Burr asks. His voice sounds impatient.

"He said we should bandage it," Landon says.

"Right. Right," Burr says. "We can use my shirt." He begins to lift his T-shirt over his head. His skin looks pale. I never realized he was so thin. His ribs wrap around his torso, bone by bone.

"Don't use your shirt," I say. "We should use Dale's."

Dale glances at me with a very surprised expression.

"Is my shirt somehow more sterile?" Dale asks.

"You've got a jacket you can wear to protect yourself from the sun. If Burr shreds his shirt he won't have anything," I say.

"She's right," Landon says.

Even adrift, I like being right.

Dale slides out of his dark blue Windbreaker and tugs his T-shirt over his head. I don't think I've ever seen him without a shirt. I assumed he'd look exactly like Wick. But there is a lot more mass to him. His pectoral muscles rise away from his body in nicely defined squares. His abs are also flat and toned. He catches me staring at him, but I'm so tired that I don't stop.

"Here," Dale says. He tosses the shirt to Burr, and it almost flops in the water.

"Careful," Burr says.

Burr immediately tears the T-shirt into strips.

"I don't need a head bandage," Skate says.

Burr keeps tearing. "Should I dunk them in the water or apply them dry?"

"I disagree with Munny," Wick says. "I think we should use the water to clean the wound. Hospitals use saline water all the time to clean wounds."

"The ocean isn't saline water. There's algae and bacteria. It could make it more septic," Munny says.

Wick responds with a forceful voice. He even points his finger at Munny. "The salt will dry the wound and help seal it."

"No, you're supposed to keep stitches clean and dry and covered," Munny says.

"We're not talking about stitches," Wick says. "It's an open wound."

"Shut up!" Burr says. "I don't need a bio-nerd showdown. I think we should clean the wound."

Munny huffs a little and looks away. "Bad idea."

Burr takes hold of Skate on his stomach and behind his head. "I'm going to lean you back. Close your eyes."

Skate laughs a little. "I feel like I'm being baptized."

Burr gently lowers Skate's head into the water. It must sting. I watch Skate's face contort in pain. He tightly grips Burr's hand at his stomach.

"It's okay," Burr says. "I've got you."

"Do you need help?" Landon asks.

"I'm good," Burr says. He lifts Skate to a seated position again.

"This stings," Skate says.

"It means it's working," Burr says.

Munny shakes his head. I catch Munny's eye, and mouth the word *Don't*. He nods and looks away. We don't need any pessimists on board. We all need to stay upbeat. Burr wraps the torn shirt around Skate's head. The green cloth presses around his hair and circles around his forehead, making him look like a warrior.

"It feels better," Skate says.

"Good," Sov says.

"Now we just need to be patient and wait," Wick says.

"Yeah," Landon says.

"We should tell stories," Wick says.

My mind clicks back to my earlier question about boats going down. I want to hear stories about survivors. If we can do what they did, we'll be okay. "What about the *Titanic*?" I ask. "How many of those people survived?"

"I saw the movie," Wick says. "I think the guy who hit the engine propeller definitely bit it."

He tries to laugh, but I ignore his joke.

"The movie was pretty accurate. A lot of people survived, right?" I ask. I open my eyes.

"These aren't the kind of stories I had in mind," Wick says.

"Dude, you can't be serious. You think any of us know the actual number of survivors aboard the *Titanic*?"

"Around seven hundred people survived," Munny says. He looks at Dale and smiles. "They were rescued by the *Carpathia*."

"Really? I feel better knowing that," I say. "Seven hundred is a lot."

"Over twice that many died," Munny says. "And the *Carpathia* itself was later torpedoed and sunk in World War I by a German U-boat. The *Snowdrop* picked up those survivors. I mean, the ones who weren't killed in the attack."

"That's so depressing," I say.

"Let's lay off torpedo references," Landon says. "Let's keep things upbeat."

"No," I say. "Let's stick with my question. I was serious. This has happened before, right? Boats like ours, small boats, they've got to sink all the time, right? People drifting in dinghies, this can't be that unusual?" I've made fists, and I'm smacking my thighs with them. I focus on looking at myself and my own body. I refuse to look into the water.

"I've read some stories," Munny says.

"Before you let loose more nautical disaster tales, do these stories have survivors?" Wick asks. "I mean, when I suggested telling stories this wasn't what I had in mind."

"Yeah," Munny says. "Some survivors."

"I want to hear," I say. "If there were some survivors, that means there's got to be a way for us to survive too."

"Well, the first story is pretty famous. A family sailing around the world in a yacht got attacked by a pod of killer whales."

"Stop. You can't be serious. I've been to SeaWorld, and Shamu licked my face. Orcas don't sink ships," Dale says.

Every time I look at Dale, all I see are his muscles. Do they give him an advantage over the rest of us? How can that be fair? Why have I never noticed them before?

"Actually, in this instance, they did. They mistook the yacht for an injured baleen mother whale. They'd already eaten her baby."

"How do killer whales sink a yacht?" Landon asks.

"They ram it with their heads until it breaks apart," Munny says.

"But they survived?" I ask.

"Yeah, the whole family made it. Their ship, the *Lucette*, sank, and they drifted for thirty-eight days until they were found by a Japanese tuna fisher."

"Dude, that's freaking impossible," Dale says.

"Not if they had fishhooks and water and a few provisions," Burr says.

"Yeah, they did," Munny says.

"They should make a movie about that," I say.

"They did," Munny says. "It starred Ali MacGraw and Robert Urich."

I don't know who those people are, so I don't say anything else.

"What's the longest anyone has survived adrift?" Burr asks after a pause.

"Well, there was this couple that wanted to sail around the world in their yacht. They made it from England almost to the Galapagos Islands. But a harpooned sperm whale attacked their yacht and sunk it. They drifted for over three months in a dinghy. That's the longest anyone has survived adrift. But they had some gear, and some drinking water. I think they made it a hundred and seventeen days."

"Dude, the Coast Guard won't let us drift out here for three shitty months," Dale says.

"You're right," Burr says. "No way that's happening."

"I'm totally against whaling," I say. I'm not surprised to hear that whales are starting to fight back.

"The couple didn't harpoon the whale," Munny said. "Another boat did, and the injured whale lashed out at their yacht by mistake."

There's silence. We're all looking at the horizon, probably each secretly hoping to see a Japanese tuna fisher and not a whale.

"There was a boat that sank off the coast of North Carolina in the eighties," Munny says. "*The Trashman*."

"I'm not picking on you," Wick says. "But how the hell do you know that?"

I'm not surprised to hear Wick needle Munny. Ever since he accidentally saw the intelligence charts a few months ago that ranked all the twins by IQ, he's been preoccupied by his listing as second-smartest twin. I don't take the rankings all that seriously, though there does seem to be some validity to them. From brightest to dimmest the studies yielded the following results: Munny, Wick, Sov, me, Landon, Burr, Skate, and Dale.

"After we read *Life of Pi* in Culture Club, I got real interested in sea disasters," Munny says. "It's called utilizing your local library in order to pursue your interests. I highly recommend it."

I ignore Munny's comment. I'm so relieved to hear about a boat like ours sinking.

"How did they all survive?" I ask.

"They didn't. Only two survived. They were found by a Russian freighter," Munny says. "Three didn't make it."

"Crap!" I say. I don't like those odds. Two out of five. Two out of five! I scan the boat. People's faces range from freaked out to disappointed. Burr gazes at the horizon. Skate keeps his bandaged head down. Dale keeps opening and closing his mouth. I think he's mouthing *son of a bitch*. Landon stares in to the bottom of the raft, while Wick gives my hand a few reassuring squeezes.

"Doesn't anybody know of a more positive boat story?" Landon asks.

There's a long silence, and I can hear small waves harmlessly licking against the rubber sides of our raft.

"Noah's ark," Skate says. His voice sounds happy but thin.

We all turn to look at Skate. His eyes are closed, and he's leaning heavily into the side of the raft.

"That's a great story for us all to think about," Landon says.

I wrinkle my face. I don't think Landon actually knows that much about the story. Other than a few funerals and one wedding, and about five months of Bible classes with my grandma when we were nine, we haven't been to church. I don't think we own a Bible.

"How long did they drift?" Landon asks.

"Forty days and forty nights," Burr says.

"And they were carrying animals, which is a burden we don't have," Landon adds.

He's acting like it's a pep rally. I half expect Landon to try to lead us in a cheer for Noah.

"After forty days and forty nights, the rain ended, and

a hundred and fifty days later the ark came to rest on the mountains of Ararat," Skate says. He licks his lips several times and continues. "Noah sent out a raven, but it didn't come back. So he sent a dove three times. The first time, the dove came back. The second time, the dove returned with an olive branch in its beak. And the third time, the dove never returned. This was the sign that the flood was over." Skate opens his eyes. His spirits seem lifted. I didn't even realize that he'd read the Bible. I thought Mormons were all hung up on their own book.

"Thanks," Landon says.

I feel like I should say something too. It took a lot of effort for Skate to tell us that story. "I really enjoyed that," I mumble.

We drift, and nobody offers another Bible tale. Nobody offers anything.

"I can't wait until this is over," Wick whispers in my ear.

"Yeah," I say.

"Yeah," Dale says. "Mom is probably pissing herself right now."

It bothers me that Dale was listening to what Wick whispered to me.

"She might not know anything about it yet," Wick says.

"The Coast Guard would have notified her by now. Right?" He directs his question at Burr. But Burr is still staring into the horizon. "Burr? Dude, I'm talking to you."

He turns his head and looks at Dale. "Yeah," he says. "I think so."

I can't be the only person who notices how unsure he sounds.

"You think so?" Dale asks.

Burr's voice grows more assertive. "I don't know all of the Coast Guard's procedures. Let's talk about something else. Let's not obsess about the Coast Guard."

"I bet our parents don't know yet," Sov says.

"The Coast Guard wouldn't know which families to notify," Munny says.

"Wouldn't they try to get in touch with the boat's owner?" Landon asks.

"My parents are listed," Burr says.

Mentioning Mr. and Mrs. Riggs makes us stop talking. I finally break the quiet. "Mom might drive down," I say to Landon. "When I don't call her back, when you don't call her back, she might figure out that I came here."

"That's true," Landon says. "I bet she does drive down."

"Wait," I say.

"What?" Landon asks.

"She might check out youth hostels or go to Canada first," I say.

I know I'm going to have to elaborate, so I do.

"At the wedding, I told her that I might drive off to Canada. It was a joke, but after I go missing she might think I was serious."

"Why would she look into youth hostels?" Landon asks.

"I was talking to this guy and I told him that I wanted

to go check into one for a week and unplug," I say.

"Okay," Landon says.

"What guy?" Wick asks.

"A wedding guest," I say.

"Even if she did drive down, she wouldn't know we took a boat out," Munny says.

He's right. Any hope I had that my mother would rescue me evaporates.

"Dude," Dale says. "I feel depressed. What should we talk about now?"

Landon jumps in. "I know. We should focus on why we want to live. It will keep us positive. With a focus on the future."

That makes sense.

"Cool idea," Burr says.

"Yeah," Skate adds.

"Like giving voice to our life-sustaining wishes," Wick says.

"Okay, let's go around and talk about all the things we still want to do. Enid, you start," Landon says.

I look at the cut on my thumb. What do I want more than anything?

"I want to go to Alaska and see glaciers," I say.

"Really?" Wick asks.

I glance at Landon's face, and he looks surprised. "The idea just came to me," I say. "Why? Do we have to justify why we want it, too?"

Landon shakes his head. "No. No explanations needed."

"Okay. You go," I say.

"I want to write a best-selling mystery. Something gritty," he says.

"You don't even read that much," I say.

"Enid, let's not challenge each other's life-sustaining wishes," Wick says.

"Fine," I say. "I didn't realize I was doing that." I think the heat is adversely affecting my ability to filter what I say during conversations.

Burr goes next, and he really comes to life. He sits up straight and speaks with an energetic enthusiasm that I haven't heard come out of him in a very long time. "I want to go on a mission to someplace cool. I hope I get sent to Russia."

Neither Skate nor Burr have talked that much about going on missions, but Burr sure seems jazzed about it right now. "The suits. The Missionary Training Center. The companions. The bicycle. The name tags. I'm ready for it."

Skate looks up and smiles. "Me too. Russia. France. Brazil. A faraway place. I want to learn a language."

I should ask him how his head is feeling. I think Burr wrapped the bandages too tight. The green cloth is cutting into Skate's skin around his temples.

"That sounds great," I say. I don't bring up the bandages. If they felt too tight, Skate would say something.

I shift so I can see Dale. He sits in the raft wearing his Windbreaker, his chest bare and growing pink from sun exposure. He looks like a hillbilly.

"I want to try cocaine," he says.

"What?" I say. "That's nuts."

"Enid, don't shoot down his wish," Wick says.

I didn't realize I'd said that out loud. My filter is definitely gone.

"What's your problem with my life-sustaining wish? Lots of people try cocaine. You go to a party. People have extra blow. You toot a little. That's all it takes, and you've tried cocaine."

"Thanks for the tutorial," I say.

"You're so high and mighty," Dale says. "I can't believe my brother enjoys dating you."

"Hey," Wick says. "Don't judge Enid."

I glare at Dale. I want to flip him off. I want to punch him in his hillbilly gut. But I don't have the energy. "I cannot believe that I'm stuck on a life raft with you." I turn away from him.

"It *is* pretty surprising considering you weren't even invited to the party," Dale says.

"Stop," Wick says. "Enid is off-limits."

The way Wick says that makes me feel that they've had conversations about me being off-limits before.

"Okay," Landon interrupts. "Let's hear from Sov and Munny."

I look at them. Their thin shirts have become so dry that they look transparent now. Not even a full day at sea, and already our clothes are wrecked.

"Munny?" Wick says.

Munny looks at Wick, then me, then Sov. Then he just

sort of stares off heavenward into nothing.

His voice is soft. "I want to learn how to play the guitar. I want to be on television. I want to kiss Dina Sneed. I want to visit San Francisco. I want to have sex. I want to eat at A Single Pebble again. I want to order the mock eel. I want to go to college. I want to look inside a volcano. I want to make a soufflé. I want to get married. I want to build my own house. I want to have kids."

"Shit, that's a whole life," Dale says.

Munny nods. "Yeah. That's what I want. A whole life."

We're quiet. We are taking it in. Thinking about the size of those words. A whole life. That's so much more than a single life-sustaining wish. Wow. He really is the smartest twin.

"Sov? What about you?" Landon encourages.

Sov smiles. "That's tough to follow."

"You've got to have something," Landon says.

"I do." Sov closes his eyes and releases a breath. "I want to learn how to play the guitar. I want to be on television. I want to kiss Dina Sneed. I want to go to San Francisco." Sov starts laughing. And he doesn't stop. He doubles over.

"You guys really have identical life plans?" Dale asks.

"He's joking," Munny says. "Okay. Get serious. What do you want?"

Sov laughs a little more and stops. He pans around the raft. "I want to start a blog. Not a blog about me. But something for the Culture Club. We've come really close to getting big names. I think if we didn't ask them

139

to travel to Vermont that we could get them to appear on our blog. And do interviews, and that would be cool."

"Cool," Landon says. "Who would you want to have on the blog?"

"Really famous literary people, like Al Young and Tobias Wolff and Amy Tan and Michael Chabon."

"That sounds like a great idea," Wick says.

"I've only heard of Amy Tan," Burr says.

"They're all famous. Trust me," Sov says.

When we're all finished saying our life-sustaining wish, we don't have another topic ready to mull over. Nobody puts anything forward. I think we're too tired. The sun is overhead beating down on us. I look back into the water. I try to swallow. But my mouth is so dry. I've never been this thirsty before in my whole life. It's a frightening feeling. I remember my first question and ask it again.

"How long can the average person go without water?" I ask.

"You really want the answer?" Munny asks. "In these conditions, not more than three days."

"Shit!" Burr says. "I thought a person could go a week."

"Not in these conditions," Munny adds.

"Why are you so upset?" Wick asks. "The Coast Guard is coming. You called them. We won't have to go three days, right?"

Burr nods. "Yeah. I'm just surprised to hear that."

"I'd rather drink the sea than my own piss," Dale says.

"That's the worst thing you can do," Sov says. "All that salt. You'll speed up the dehydration. Your kidneys will shut down."

"I don't want to know this," Dale says.

Another large wave comes, and we're all tense, trying to position our weight in a way that will keep the raft steady. The fins are still there. The sharks are back. They circle relentlessly, bumping and nudging the raft.

"Can I lie down?" Skate asks. "I feel dizzy."

"Sure," Burr says. "Stretch out."

Skate lies down in the bottom of the raft. Even bandaged, his head looks like it has begun bleeding again. He rests it on the floor of the raft and blood stains the water that collected there.

"Do you think that's why the sharks are here? Because of his head?" Dale asks.

"No. Shut up," Burr says.

"And look at her hand," Dale says, pointing to me.

I'd forgotten all about my cut. It isn't that big. It's a small gash underneath my thumb.

"You guys are bleeding in the water," Dale says. "You're leaving a blood trail."

"We are not," I say.

"Oh my God," Dale says. "It's like you're on the same team as the sharks. You're luring them to us."

"Shut up," Landon says. "The sharks are here because they're sharks."

"And because we've got two people with open wounds," Dale says.

"I doubt that's the spirit with which Noah steered the ark," I say.

Burr lifts his arm up and interrupts us. "Man, is that the Coast Guard?"

We all excitedly turn our heads. Relief washes over me. I can feel my heart beating in my ears.

"Where?" Wick asks.

"Right there," Burr says.

He's pointing to a shadow on the water made by a rogue cloud.

"Dude, that's not anything," Dale says.

"It's a shadow," Munny says.

Our excitement is replaced by tangible disappointment. My heartbeat continues to drum. The beats turn into a pulse and the pulse begins to ache.

"Do not say you see the Coast Guard unless you're totally sure," Dale says.

"It could have been something," Landon offers.

I nod. I watch the shadow, secretly hoping that it will somehow turn into a ship. But once the sun emerges again, that spot becomes nothing but a patch of regular seawater.

"It could have been something," Landon repeats.

We're all watching that spot as we drift farther out to sea. The sharks continue their patrol. We're getting a bit more used to them. I've gone so far as to name three of them: Notch, Chip, and Belly. Notch has a chunk of flesh missing from his dorsal fin. Chip's nose is pocked by several deep scars. And Belly likes to approach our raft and turn on his side, revealing his white underside. I guess I think that if I name them, I can somehow tame them. I wonder if this is how people who work with lions feel. You've got to feel like you know an animal before you can stick your head in its mouth. I want these sharks to become familiar to me. Maybe the others will hurt me, but not Notch, Chip, or Belly. Not that I plan on sticking my head in their mouths.

I close my eyes and try to think about something other than sharks. My mind drifts to my father and all the mistakes he's made. Even if my mother can, I'm never going to be able to forgive him. He didn't just have one affair; he had three. How can a man do that? Three times? Three different women?

Then I think of my own mistake, that heartless thing I did before I left Vermont. I didn't mean to hurt that girl. When I called her, I didn't mean to say what I said to her. I look into the empty sky. It would feel so good to see a dove, or any bird at all. My own pulse continues to beat painfully in my head. I put it down and start to cry. But, like Burr, I'm so dehydrated that there's just a sound, and no actual tears come.

chapter 13

I'm surprised that I'm able to sleep for such long stretches on the raft. But when a body gets exhausted, I guess anywhere will do. I wake up and I'm sitting on the floor, my head cradled in Wick's lap. Wick softly strokes the nape of my neck. I look up into his face. His chin and cheeks are dark with stubble. Seeing him this way makes him look unfamiliar, a different kind of sexy. I reach up and touch his face. It feels unshaved and rough.

"How are you?" he asks.

"Fine," I say.

"Do you need anything?"

"A snow cone," I say. "And ten dollars."

He laughs. He loves my sense of humor, and it makes me happy to have this sort of ability. Even in a moment like this, I have the power to draw laughter out of him.

"I'll get right on that," he says.

He strokes my neck again and leans down and kisses my ear. His lips feel like cardboard.

"If you want to switch places and rest in my lap we can do that," I say.

"Maybe in a little bit," he says.

My head feels weightless in his lap. This is how we watch movies together. We take turns holding each other.

I want things to be like they were with Wick. I know he called me his girlfriend. But what if that means that he only feels that way right now? What happens once we get off the raft?

Anxiety starts to spin through me. I can't even enjoy the closeness right now. No longer throbbing, my head is buzzing. I feel like Wick and I need to have a conversation. The thought of our reconciliation being temporary consumes me. I want to know how he feels. I want him to extinguish all the chaos that I'm feeling. But I don't want to push him away.

"I've never been in water this deep," I say.

"Yeah," Wick says. "I have no idea how far down it is to the bottom. Maybe miles."

I release the grip on his hand and lightly stroke his arm. "I'm glad we're here together." I lift my head off of him and sit up. I lean against him, nuzzle his chest. When I do this I glance across the raft and notice Landon. He's mouthing a word to me. What is he saying? I focus on his lips: *Space*. I turn my face into Wick's chest. I don't want to give Wick space. Those are the old rules. They don't apply on the raft. Wick doesn't even appear to want space. I think he wants me.

I am about to say something else to Wick when Dale interrupts everything.

"I need to take a piss," he says.

"What are you going to do?" Wick asks.

I do not want to witness Dale drink his own pee.

Dale holds his head in his hands. "Shit. If I do this,

nobody can ever tell anybody."

We are all awake and looking at Dale. He sits on the side of the raft chewing on his bottom lip, staring at his crotch. "Won't it make me sick?"

Munny shakes his head.

"Enid, close your eyes," Dale says.

"No problem," I say.

I hear the sound of him unzipping his pants.

"You could pee into your jacket," Sov says. "Make a little bowl and then drink from that."

I hear the sound of Wick peeling himself out of his Windbreaker.

"Put it in your hand like this," Sov says.

"Don't worry about any of us telling anybody," Wick says. "This is a life and death situation."

Dale releases an anguished scream. The next thing I hear is the sound of a small trickle of liquid hitting the ocean. It doesn't last long.

"You can open your eyes now," Wick says.

I open them and I see Dale's back to me. He peed into the ocean. I'm not surprised. I'm not sure I could drink my urine either.

"This is a sick situation," Dale says.

I don't disagree. I resettle my head on Wick's lap and drop the conversation. I want reassurance about the future, but this is fine for now. Things feel good. What I have is enough. Isn't it? "Tell me when you want it to be your turn," I say.

Wick lovingly pets my head. "Sure thing."

"Don't sleep too much," Landon says.

"Yeah," I say. But what does he mean by that? In our current conditions, how is it possible to sleep too much? It's the most pleasant way to pass the time.

Every time I open my eyes, I blink and blink. My eyesight has a hard time adjusting to the day. The light feels so strong. I worry that after this experience, after we're rescued, I might have to get glasses. Maybe sea glare damages your pupils or corneas. This thought makes me so sad. I don't want to be permanently injured by all this. I want to stay who I am and return to my life exactly as I was. I consider slipping back to sleep.

I thought we'd be rescued by now. We're all basically good people on this raft. There's no need for us to be out here, still drifting. I feel like any lesson we were supposed to have learned, we've gotten. Personally, I've been cured of that whole I-wish-my-life-were-more-interesting attitude I had earlier. My life is fine. I want it back. What's happening is worse than any nightmare I've ever had. It's worse than any nightmare I can imagine. Beyond the sharks. Beyond the thirst. And in addition to the softening raft, there's this awful smell. In addition to everything else that's gone disastrously wrong, I'm sitting in a puddle of disgusting water. It's a combination of seawater, blood, pus, and—I'm embarrassed to admit—urine. I had to pee in the boat. There was no way I could drink mine either. I didn't even mention it to anybody.

And after discovering the sharks, there was no way I was willing to risk clamoring near the raft's edge, like Dale, even for that. Besides, if I tried to pee off the side . . . I'm a girl; I lack the necessary equipment to do that sort of thing from a reasonably safe distance. But I'm not the only one. Skate has gotten weaker. He's relieved himself in the raft too.

Every time I look into the sky I expect to see a bird; not necessarily a dove, but maybe a gull. It's like they don't exist anymore. Up there, it's an endless blue; the clouds are gone and there is nothing. Except that hot, glaring sun. I always knew that the sun was a burning ball of flames, but it never truly felt like that until now. It turns the sea a painful golden color. Sometimes, because of the way the light strikes it, the water looks solid, and I have to remind myself that yes, it's really liquid out there. Yes, Enid, you and the guys, for the time being, are completely screwed.

"Are you okay?" Wick asks me.

"I guess," I say.

Even though there are six other people on the raft, they seem to have zoned out. It's as if Wick and I are all alone right now, having a private conversation.

"It's surreal that you're here," he says.

"You're glad, right?" I ask.

"I am and I'm not. I wish you were safe," he says.

"I wish we were both safe. I wish we were all safe," I say.

"Can I ask you a question?" Wick says.

"Yeah," I say.

"So why are you here?"

I don't feel like being honest right now. I don't want to start talking about how I doubted Wick's truthfulness. About how I suspected Simone was going to be here. I think all that stuff makes me look bad. And desperate. Also, it doesn't feel important anymore. The truth about why I'm here feels so lame and insignificant. I try a different tack. One designed to test his feelings for me.

"I wasn't sure if you were serious about dating other people," I say.

There is a long pause. He outlines my ear with his finger. With my head in his lap, I can't see his face and he can't see mine.

"I never said we should date other people. I don't want you dating somebody else."

This makes me feel better. But I still press him. I want total clarity. I want to reinstate our relationship and know that it will remain reinstated after we return to our real lives.

"I thought you said we were on a break," I say.

"That doesn't mean date other people," he says.

"Oh."

"Enid, I really like you. Things were really great for a long time," he says.

I realize he's using the past tense in referring to our relationship, and I don't know if that's intentional or he's become dehydrated to the point of losing his ability to articulate his feelings. I root for the latter.

"Things can still be good. Once we get back," I say.

Wick stops tracing my ear. "I don't want to hurt your feelings," he says. "But there were some serious things wrong with our relationship."

My whole body whirs with disappointment. I sit up and look at him. We look into each other's eyes. Our cheeks are sunburned. Our noses are completely red and peeling. "No relationship is perfect." I think that's something my mom actually repeats to herself when gearing up to face my father.

"When you found out about your dad's last affair, after you learned about everything, you became really anxious about our relationship," Wick says.

I want to deny this. But I know I should listen to what he's saying.

"All men aren't like your father. I'm not like him. But you were so aggressively insecure. I felt really judged. Like everything I did and said was under constant scrutiny. And it made it hard for me to want to be around you."

I feel awful. I did get more needy after my dad's recent revelations. But what am I supposed to do? It's hard to trust people after you've been hurt. Over and over.

"I'm sorry," I say.

"I'm not looking for an apology," he says. "I'm trying to explain things."

"Right," I say.

"You were constantly checking my phone and e-mails. You wanted to read all my papers, which at first was cool because I thought you were looking for typos, but then it felt like you were dissecting them. Like you distrusted me so much you were hunting for signs of infidelity in my response papers to George Eliot."

I feel so humiliated. He really could have stopped expounding on his reasons for dumping me after the "aggressively insecure" comment.

"I get it," I say. "Okay."

"You don't get it," he says.

I push away from him and sit in a position where no part of my body is touching any part of his body, even our shoulders. I give him space.

"I love you, Enid. But you became impossible," Wick says.

I stop breathing. Is there a way for me to become un-impossible?

"I love you too," I say.

The silence drags. I look out into the water, and it goes on and on. The length of the horizon feels like the length of my sadness. Wick reaches down and touches my leg. "I think we can work on stuff."

This is exactly what I want to hear. With everything else going on in my life right now, I want to have things with Wick go right. We're going to be a couple again. In fact, we're a couple right now. Don't I deserve this?

"That's what I want too," I say.

He keeps holding my leg. I look at his hand and then I look at him. He's staring at Skate sleeping on the floor of the raft.

Wick nudges Skate's shoulder with his sneaker. "Hey,

big guy," Wick says. "Do you want to sit up for a little bit?"

Skate opens his eyes. He shivers in the fetid water pooling around him.

"Sit up here," I say. I slide over and make room.

Wick pulls Skate up. Landon and Dale help. They ease him onto the raft's sidewall next to me.

"It's easy to just conk out," Skate says.

"Yeah," I say.

I take my arm and put it around Skate's waist to help keep him steady. I feel Wick's arm reach around and touch mine.

Wick leans forward and says, "I'm glad you're here."

I lean forward and say, "That's very selfish of you."

"Sometimes, I'm a totally selfish guy," he says.

Before Wick and I can intensify our flirtation, Dale interrupts us.

"Guys, I just endured hearing you two rehash all your relationship issues. I can only take so much. Can you please not turn the experience into a romance novel?"

"That was a private conversation," I say.

"You're in a raft with me. Where do you want me to go? The waiting room?"

"Stop, Dale," Wick says.

"Dude, I'm totally allowed to contribute my feelings. You can't silence me."

Things were going so well. But not anymore. That's the kind of energy Dale possesses. Wrecking-ball energy. I am so tired. So sick of Dale. I want to insult him, but my mind struggles to remember nouns.

"You're acting like a real Sandinista," I say.

"A sandy what? Did you just call me an asshole in a foreign language?"

"No," Munny says. "She said Sandinista, a member of a Nicaraguan left-wing political party. Also, it's an album by The Clash."

"I know," Dale says.

"No you didn't," I say. "You're the eighth smartest person on this raft. That makes you the most dumb." I have no idea why I called him a Sandinista, but I don't back away from it.

"Enid, don't," Wick says.

"Well, you're the most crazy," Dale says.

"I'm not crazy," I say.

"Nobody said you were," Landon says.

"Landon, he said I was the most—"

"I know. He didn't mean it," Landon says.

"Yeah, dude, I didn't mean it."

I shouldn't pick on Dale's intelligence. I know it really wounds him. Why can't I be a bigger person? Why do I have to react so much to people?

"I think I want to rest again," Skate says.

He lowers himself back to the raft's floor.

"Okay," Wick says. "But let's keep your head up and out of that water."

"Sure thing," Skate says. He sits down and leans his head back on the raft's side. His head touches my leg. I can see pus escaping through the crease of the green bandage. "I think I'm going to rest some more," he says again.

"Good idea," I say. But I do not know if it really is a good idea. I wonder what he thinks about when he sleeps? I wonder if he dreams about his parents? Now that they're dead, I wonder where he thinks they are?

I look into the sky. There are no clouds. It's blank. Back when my father and I used to talk, he told me that when you skydive, you want to avoid clouds. They contain hidden dangers. I imagine my father falling out of the empty sky right now. A speck tumbling toward me. But then I blink and he's not there anymore. It's just the sky. My grandmother used to call the sky the heavens. In my head, I repeat that word over and over. *Heaven. Heaven. Heaven.*

"There is so much goddamned water in the world," Wick says.

"I was just thinking that," Landon says.

"I was thinking about heaven," I say.

"You were?" Landon asks.

"Yeah, I think I believe in God."

"That came out of left field," Landon says.

"Of course you believe in God. You're in a raft surrounded by sharks. I bet you've started believing in Jesus, too."

"Historically speaking, Jesus was an actual person," Munny says. "I don't think belief is the right word."

"You know so much unimportant junk that it's impossible to like you," Dale says.

154

"I like Munny," I say. "And I've been thinking about God for a while. Not just today. Two days ago I was totally thinking about Moses."

"You were?" Landon asks.

"Yeah. Why, were you thinking about him too?" I ask. I'm always hoping that our twin connection will kick in.

"No," Landon says. "I just didn't realize that nonreligious teenagers sporadically thought about Moses."

"That is a little weird," Wick says. "What exactly were you thinking about?"

I don't want to mention thinking of the bulrushes story when I took the directions from Landon's basket. So I lie.

"How he fought Goliath," I say.

"That was David. Even I know that, and that's saying something," Dale says. "I may be a Christian, but at this point in my life, I care about the Bible about as much as I care about Canada."

"What do you have against Canada?" Sov asks. "I have relatives that live there."

"So do we," Wick says.

Dale doesn't answer.

"All I was trying to say is that I believe in God. And I think we're going to be okay," I say. "I think saving the llama got me thinking about these deeper issues."

"That thing died," Dale says.

"I know," I say. "*That* got me thinking about even deeper issues."

Wick rubs my knee. Talking about God makes me feel hopeful. I wonder if I'll care about these things after

I'm rescued. Am I the type of person who wants to go to church? Every week? I don't know. I can't imagine myself sitting on a pew that many times per month. I turn to look into the water.

"Hey, what's that?" I ask.

"Do you see a ship?" asks Landon.

"No, that right there. That white thing. It looks like my shoe."

"That's not possible," Landon says.

"But it totally looks like my white pump."

"It's something. It could be a piece of Styrofoam. Or some other piece of trash. It's too far away," Wick says.

"Let's row toward it," I say. I reach my arm into the ocean.

"There's sharks in there, Enid," Sov says.

I pull my hand back in the raft. "I want my shoe," I say.

"Dude, get over it," Dale says.

"Dude, if it were your shoe and you were barefooted, you'd want it too," I say.

Dale shrugs.

"It's drifting toward us," Munny says. "We'll probably intercept it."

I clutch my heart. "I hope we do," I say.

"Enid, it's just a shoe," Wick says.

"I know. But it's my mother's."

"When you tell her the story of what happened to it, I'm sure she won't care that you lost it," Wick says.

"But I'll care."

I don't know why, but my mother's shoe has taken on all this extra meaning. I sit and wait. The shoe bobs merrily along. Eventually, it drifts so close that Landon is able to lean over the side and pluck it from the sea.

"Enjoy," he says, tossing it to me.

"I don't believe it! Where are those Doritos bags?" Dale asks.

"Get over the chips," Landon says.

I try to slide the shoe on, but my foot is swollen. It hurts. I decide just to hold it.

"Thanks," I say.

"Any time," Landon says. "But I wouldn't expect to come across your other pump. Cherish the one you have."

I press it to my chest and lean back into Wick's arms. I think that I'm going to stay awake and be responsible and totally look for passing ships, but I feel myself dozing off instead.

chapter 14

The raft is developing a crust of salt. The sun evaporates the water, and in the creases of the rubber, the salt hangs on. I hate the salt. It's become an enemy. I try not to look at it. I'm almost happy when the ocean laps at the salt pockets, dissolving them back into the sea. My throat aches, and more than anything else in the world, I want water. I look at my hand. The small wound has become infected. I can see yellow pus surrounding the gash. I touch it.

"Does it hurt?" Landon asks.

He's seated at the other end of raft. He's perched on a side, which requires more balance, but it keeps him elevated above the floor. He's been watching me.

"It hurts a little," I say. "But I'll be fine."

"I know you will," he says.

I want to ask him how much he drank. Sores are breaking out on his face and arms. I'm worried that he's going to become dehydrated faster than the rest of us. Why were the guys drinking at all? That was so stupid. I look away from Landon. Next to him is Burr, seated beside Skate. Anger floods over me when I look at Burr and Skate. This is all their fault. I hate them. It was their party. It was their ship. It was their beer. It was their stupidity. Burr sees me watching him.

"What?" he asks. "Why are you looking at me like that?"

I turn to face the water.

"What's wrong with you?" Burr asks. His voice is thinner than usual and very tense.

"I wasn't looking at you," I say.

"You totally were staring at Burr. I saw you," Dale says.

I shrug my shoulders.

"Sorry," I say.

I continue to watch the water. Everybody's nerves are on edge. I need to be careful. I've taken two semesters of psychology, and I know that under the right conditions, anybody can lose it. Under duress, anybody has the potential to become dangerous. And this is duress to the nth degree.

"The Coast Guard will be here before nightfall," Burr says.

"You think so?" Wick asks.

"I'm sure of it," Burr says. "If there's one thing you can count on in life, it's the Coast Guard."

Skate moans, and Burr tries to soothe him by rubbing his shoulder. Skate sleeps more than he's awake. His head isn't bleeding anymore, but the wound is infected. I think back to the gash before Burr wrapped it. It's worse than the cut on my hand. Like the kind of wound you'd expect to see on a death-marked character in a movie about the apocalypse, not the kind of injury you'd expect to see blooming on the back of your childhood friend's head. He needs antibiotics. He needs a doctor. But these things are hours and hours and hours away. I don't want my mind to arrive at this, but it does. Without medical attention, without water, how many hours does Skate have left? I feel sad and helpless. I've arrived at a level of despair that is lower than anything I've ever felt.

I imagine that my mind is a television and I turn it to another channel. After spending a few minutes looking at my thumb, trying to will it to heal itself, I turn to the water again. I see something. It's floating next to the raft and looks like a heap of garbage. I set my shoe beside me and lean over the side. I think it's seaweed. I reach carefully, snatch up a fibrous bundle of it, and pull a dripping line on board.

"What are you doing?" Dale asks. "What are you putting in the raft?"

"Can we eat it?" I ask Munny. It has the appearance of canned spinach mixed with large grapes, except it's much tougher and browned.

"It's full of salt," Munny says. "It would dehydrate us."

I'm holding the messy rope of seaweed in my arms. It's hard for me to put it back in the ocean. Then, an orange leaf of it breaks off and plops on the raft's bottom. The leaf sprouts legs and begins rowing itself sideways toward my foot. It's a crab. I scream. I don't scream because I'm afraid of it, but because I wasn't expecting it.

"Get it out of the raft," Dale says.

"Enid, toss it over," Landon says. "It's sargassum weed and it's full of sargasso crabs."

Then, as if it were possible to rain tender, damp crabs, the seaweed releases a dozen of them. They drip onto the raft's floor and begin to swim toward our legs. I guess they're looking for cover. I reach down and pick up the one closest to my foot. I pinch its body between my thumb and index finger. "This crap is full of them," Burr says.

"Wait, isn't sargasso weed what Atlantic Ridley sea turtles swim to after they're born? We could eat sea turtles," Munny says.

His comment jogs my mind. On a trip to Florida with my family, at an aquarium, Landon and I learned all about the endangered Ridley sea turtles. After hatching from eggs on shore, they leave the beach and swim out to sea. They spend the first year or more of their lives drifting in the sargassum rafts that gather in the Gulf Stream. Munny reaches into the sea and grabs for more of the brown weed. There aren't any turtles.

"Drink my own pee. Eat live turtles. I can't do this," Dale says.

I'm a little relieved that Munny doesn't find any. Ridley turtles are endangered, and I wouldn't feel comfortable eating a protected species.

"They look like grapes," Landon says, fingering a cluster of gas-filled bladders.

"Get it off the raft," Burr says. He flings another crab out to sea.

"Wait," Munny says. "We might be able to eat those."

I'm still holding a sargasso crab between my fingertips. I drop it onto the floor and watch it wriggle in the water, trying to acclimate to its own buoyancy. It reminds me of a spider, one of God's worst creations.

"Live crabs?" Dale asks.

"We can do this," Wick says.

I nod my head. "Right."

We've passed through the patch of seaweed, and it's really too late to reconsider grabbing more, so we focus on the small crabs that remain swimming in the raft. We fish through the raft water with our hands and pick them up.

"But they've been in the crap water," Dale says.

"Just eat it," Wick says.

"Wait," Landon says. "Does everybody have one?"

"Skate doesn't have one," Burr says. "I'll give him mine."

"No," Dale says. "I've got two."

How Dale went from decrying that he'd never eat a crab to become the sole person holding two both surprises me and does not surprise me.

"Give me your hand," Dale says.

Skate lifts his hand and it trembles. The flesh around his fingernails is white. The seawater is rotting our skin; it's dissolving us. And Skate looks worse than any of us.

"Just put it in his mouth," Burr says.

Skate opens his mouth and Dale delivers the crab to his awaiting tongue.

"Should I kill it first?" Dale asks.

"Pinch it hard and it will die," I say. How did I know that? How did I suddenly become a dispenser of knowledge for how to kill crabs and feed them to your friends?

Dale pinches the crab and a clear fluid runs down his thumb. Dale quickly lifts his hand to his mouth and catches the drip. "Son of a bitch, it's salt." He lowers the crab to Skate's open mouth and flicks it onto his tongue. Skate closes his mouth and chews.

"Good job," Burr says.

Once Skate is fed, I hurry to eat my own crab. I don't kill mine before I put it in my mouth. It moves across my teeth and it cracks when I bite it. It doesn't taste like anything. My mouth isn't making saliva. It's hard to chew. It's hard to swallow. My teeth are sore. So are my gums. I wish I were eating pudding.

"I'm bleeding," Dale says. He opens his mouth and blood stains his teeth.

"We're dehydrated," Munny says.

"Jesus, eating these crabs was a rotten idea." Dale points his finger at me. "Don't tell me what to do ever again."

"Don't yell at Enid," Wick says.

"We're eating seaweed and crabs," Dale says. "It's gonna kill us."

"We're not eating the seaweed," Sov says.

"Could everybody just shut up for five seconds so I can have time to think!" Burr says.

I wasn't expecting this explosion of anger from him. I stop breathing. He glares so hard at Sov that it makes me uncomfortable and I turn away. I see a fin lowering itself below the surface. I had no idea there were this many sharks left in the world.

"That seaweed brought more water on board." Burr kicks at the water gathered in the raft. "Skate can't sit in the corrosive crap. Ask before you haul anything else on the raft. Can you do that, Enid?"

I nod. I don't know why Burr is so mad at me. We all were able to eat a crab because of what I did. I look at everyone else's face. Sov and Munny are staring into the water. Landon looks at me and weakly smiles. Dale is focused on his own mouth, touching it with his fingers, checking them for blood. Skate's head droops onto his chest. I think he's asleep. Wick takes my hand and squeezes it. I don't turn to look at him. I think if I did, it would make me cry. Not that I actually could.

I can't make sense of Burr's anger. The rage behind what he says stings me, and I feel like I'm absorbing a punch. I knew Dale had anger issues, but not Burr. Learning this makes him feel like a stranger to me. I try to think of him as the version I know. If I do that, I'm not afraid of him. I know the "twin group," and they are all good guys. Burr and Skate may have their problems. Dale, of course, is a total ass, but nobody in our group would hurt me. Or themselves. Or anybody else. Not intentionally.

I wonder when our parents will know that anyone besides me is missing? Will the Coast Guard tell them? The guys aren't expected back for three more days, but my mother will be tearing apart the world to find me. She knows me. Eventually she'll figure out that I didn't drive to Canada or check into a youth hostel. She'll realize what I did and she'll drive down looking for me. She'll drive to Burr and Skate's uncle's house. He'll be the one who tells her we took the boat out. Wait! How come none of us have thought of this? He had to see that the boat was missing. When the guys didn't come back, he had to put two and two together. He must have called the Coast Guard. They *are* looking for us.

I lift my head. I can't wait to tell the guys. "The uncle!"

"What?" Wick asks.

"Burr and Skate's uncle. When you guys didn't come back, he must have looked for you. I bet he went to the dock and saw the empty slip. He must have called the Coast Guard." I reach down and touch Wick's hand. Energy I didn't know I had surges through me. I am so happy. I smile. I have hope again.

But nobody else seems the least bit excited by my revelation.

"Their uncle Bennett is out of town," Dale says softly. "He won't be back for another week."

I tumble down my ladder of happiness and fall lower than I was before. Wick squeezes my hand, but it hurts my thumb and I pull away.

"You guys were lying about staying with the uncle?" I ask. "Mom would never have let you come if she knew you were down here with zero adult supervision."

"Which was sort of the point of the lie," Dale says.

"The Coast Guard is looking for us even without Uncle Bennett," Landon says.

"Yeah," Burr says. "I gave them our coordinates. But it's like looking for a needle in a haystack."

Even with our coordinates? I think. I study Burr's expression. He doesn't look nervous. He looks tired.

"No!" Landon yells.

Notch rams the side of the raft hard, almost dumping us into the ocean. I want to think that he's just curious. But every time the fish approaches us, his tight jaws loosen and I can see rows and rows of teeth. But what's most disturbing is the way he looks at us. Right before Notch strikes us, a third lid slips down to protect his hollow-looking eyes. They're solid black, and there's no feeling there. He's just a hungry mouth attached to some fins.

"I hate their eyes," I say.

"They have a nictitating membrane to protect them when they attack," Munny says.

"I know. I can see it," I say.

Before I even know what I'm doing, I take my shoe and pitch it at Notch. It bounces off his flat head. It floats for a moment, ducklike, and then Notch opens his mouth, dives on top of it, and takes it under. The water where Notch went down foams a pale blue.

"What the hell?" Burr asks. "Don't tempt them."

"Dude, that's messed up," Dale says.

"Leave her alone," Wick says. "It's okay, Enid."

"Why did you do that?" Landon asks.

"I don't know," I say.

I fold my arms and bow my head like I'm going to pray. Notch resurfaces and rubs against the raft. If I wanted to, if any of us wanted to, we could reach out and touch his rough gray skin.

"Dude, no more messing with the sharks," Dale says.

"She won't do it again. Will you, Enid?" Landon asks.

I shake my head no. Wick rubs the back of my neck and tells me again that it's okay. But it's not okay. I look at my bare feet. They're submerged in the raft's filthy water. I wished that I hadn't thrown away my only shoe. Even if it was an impractical pump, it was something. I'm so tired, I let my hand go slack and I lose Wick's grip. I think of the road signs I passed on the drive down from Vermont. MARYLAND CHERISHES ITS WATERSHEDS and NO ILLEGAL DUMPING. $25,000 FINE. I just illegally dumped my shoe. That's a $25,000 offense. Why did I do that? Then the answer hits me, and I feel like I'm going to be sick. I threw my shoe because I'm going crazy. I'm losing it. I could be the first one to die.

Landon has moved to be by my side. I'm now flanked by him and Wick, and this makes me feel better. We're all barefoot. The guys finally decided to take off their shoes. They sit in a pile next to Skate. I wish there was a way a shoe could be useful. But shoes really only work as footwear.

"We should use the twenties to make another cash rope," Wick says.

Landon doesn't look at him. "Okay."

"You've got the twenties," Wick says.

Landon reaches into his jeans and pulls out two wadded bills. I should suggest using the shoelaces, but I don't want another argument with Dale about lace worth and possible deserted islands.

"I want to take a nap," I say. I am so tired.

"Stay awake," Landon says. "Help me fish."

"I want sleep," I say.

Landon doesn't argue with me. But I think maybe he's right. Maybe I should try to stay awake.

"My life is suck," Dale says. He looks at me. "Your life is suck."

He is so depressing.

Burr is still crouched beside Skate. Skate is awake less

than I am. He's only conscious for brief moments. To get him and his head wound out of the contaminated water, he's now sitting up all the time. Burr doesn't let him sleep on the bottom of the raft. His head is still wrapped in Dale's T-shirt, hiding the gash, and I'm glad for this, but I've spotted a new injury on him.

It's his ear. He must have hurt it when Wick threw him off *Gretchen*. As he fell, I saw him bump into the ship's side, but I hadn't noticed his ear until now. There's a big cut behind it, and it's also infected. I worry that gangrene is going to set in, that once we get him to a hospital, the ear is going to be cut off. I guess it's not the end of the world. But I'm afraid that it is the end of his ear. I bet people will start calling him Vincent van Gogh, which will be totally appropriate, Skate being the artistic type.

My hand isn't getting any better either. It's puffy and it hurts. Also, my legs are starting to grow sores. I think it's from the exposure. The sun and the salt water are corroding my skin. Actually, we all have these sores. I'm the one whose legs lack any protection at all. Why did I show up in a skirt? I'll never wear such impractical clothes again. I close my eyes and turn in to myself. We're drifting in silence again. The sun is setting. Our world is going to grow cold and dark.

"His ear is so messed up," Dale says.

"Shut up," Burr says. "He's sleeping."

But Skate's eyes are wide open; he's awake. Burr tugs at his own ear.

"It'll be okay," Burr says. "It's not that bad."

Wick is sitting on the other side of Landon.

"Where the hell is the Coast Guard?" Wick asks.

"They'll come," Burr says.

I hold my head in my hands. I wish so badly that I wasn't here. I wish I was in Vermont. I wish I was drinking water.

"We should always have someone stay awake," Wick says. "So that we can signal them."

"With what?" Dale asks. "It's going to be dark out."

Dale's comment quiets everybody.

"They'll be here," Burr says.

"I think I need a doctor," Skate says. "I'm probably gonna have to get to the hospital as soon as we get back."

"Yeah, the Coast Guard will have medics. Then you'll be taken immediately to a hospital. You'll be fine. Hang in there," Burr says.

Burr tugs at his ear again. He also rubs the back of his own head. I wonder if he can feel Skate's pain. Because of all the twin studies, I'm sure that he can. Burr looks totally wiped. I look at him and smile, but he doesn't smile back. A small wave lifts the raft, and we work to steady it. Then a large shark strikes the side of the raft, and I scream.

"Don't do that. We don't want to encourage it," Dale says.

"Actually, I don't think screaming encourages them," Munny says. "Sharks follow the electrical currents of other animals. They don't have ears. They have sensor receptors."

"Thanks for the science lesson," Dale says. "But that

doesn't explain why sharks love blood."

"They have excellent olfactory senses," Munny explains. "Their very sensitive noses can detect blood for up to a mile, as little as one part per million of blood in seawater."

"Not every species," Wick says. "You're talking about sharks like they're all identical. A dogfish shark isn't the same as a bull shark or a whale shark."

"I know that," Munny said. "I'm talking about blood—"

Wick cuts him off. "You're oversimplifying everything."

I reach out and touch Wick's arm. We don't need to bite each other's heads off.

"Dude, my brother's right," Dale says. "You're like a fact box. *I'm Munny. Here's a fact. And a fact. And a fact.*"

To further antagonize Munny, Dale makes his voice sound whiny and obnoxious.

"And you're like an empty box," Munny says. "*I didn't study. I didn't read it. Me hate knowledge. I never know answer.*"

Munny exaggerates Dale's voice, making him sound like a grunting caveman. I think it's funny, but Dale looks furious.

"Say that again and I'll punch you," Dale says.

"Don't threaten Munny," I say.

"Don't tell me what to do," Dale says. "I'm not Wick."

"She's off-limits," Wick says.

"I can say what I want to say," I say. My voice sounds strong.

"Chill out, Enid," Landon says.

I can't believe it. Landon is siding with Dale. I'm stirred awake even more.

"I hate sharks," Dale says. "I hope they all go extinct."

I see a chance to dig at him, and I take it. "Only a stupid person would say they want an entire species to go extinct. Throw the ecosystem off, and we're all doomed."

"I agree," Munny says.

"Enid," Landon says. "Shhh."

I can't believe my own brother is shushing me. I'm right.

"Let's mellow out," Landon says.

"I am mellow!" I say.

"Maybe I wasn't talking to you," Landon says.

I'm confused. Why is he being so mean to me? I can't hold in my frustration anymore. "Why is everybody on this raft starting to act like either an idiot or a jerk?"

"I haven't said anything," Sov says.

"Stop calling me stupid!" Dale says. "You think I don't know what those twin tests say? You think I don't know they think I'm the dumbest? Do you think it's fun to hear that every month of your life? Shut up!"

"She didn't call you stupid," Munny says. "She thought your comment was stupid."

"I am not stupid!" Dale picks up a shoe from the pile and throws it hard at Munny's head. The toe-end makes contact with Munny's cheekbone and bounces into the water. Munny doesn't scream, but the area underneath his eye immediately becomes red. He lifts his hand to his cheek. He looks surprised.

"Hey! You can't attack people on the life raft," I say. "That's insane!"

"Don't do that again," Landon says. "Are you okay, Munny?"

"I'm fine."

"I'm sorry. I didn't mean to hurt anybody," Dale says. "In a normal situation I wouldn't have done that. This is so messed up." He squeezes his eyes shut.

"Buckle down," Wick says. He reaches into the water to pick up the shoe, but a snapping jaw filled with teeth breaks the water's surface and engulfs the sneaker.

"Holy shit!" Wick yells.

He pulls his arm back fast, and the shark turns, slapping its tail against the side of our raft. A wave of seawater floods over us as one whole side of the raft bends upward. Landon is near the part that bows. For a second, it looks like he could tip either way. Into the water? Into the raft? He falls into the bottom of the raft, landing on his hands and knees in the cruddy water.

"Sorry," Dale says. "Sorry."

"Pull that again and I'll throw you over," Landon says. As he reseats himself, I notice that he's shaking. He could have died. He's sitting next to me, and I touch his leg. Then I release a big breath. I didn't even realize that I'd been holding my breath.

"I'm so thirsty," Burr says. "I need water."

"If we catch a fish we can eat its eyes," Munny says. "They contain water."

"How do you know that?" Burr asks.

"It's just a fact," Munny says. "I'm a fact box."

I look into the ocean. Everything is growing dark. Far off, I think I see a gray mark inching along the horizon line. Maybe it's my imagination. Maybe it's another shadow.

"Is that a ship?" I ask. My voice is quiet, almost like I'm afraid to be heard.

"Where?" Wick asks.

"There," I say, pointing.

"It is," Wick says. "Enid sees a ship!"

We're all looking at the small gray block.

"Is it the Coast Guard?" Landon asks.

"No, the Coast Guard has white ships. And there would be searchlights panning the water," Burr says. "It looks like a big fishing boat."

"Is it coming toward us? Will it see us?" I ask.

"It's going the other way," Dale says.

"Are you sure?" I ask. I don't know if it's just my imagination, or if it's the actual shape of the ship, but I think the mark looks like the silhouette of a rhinoceros. And not just any rhinoceros: the Sumatran rhino, of which there are fewer than four hundred remaining in the world. Something on the front end of it protrudes like two pointed horns, and its backside is quite broad.

It slinks along, probably ambling its way to a watering hole or another rhino. It's the smallest rhinoceros with two horns. It seems to know that it's rare. It's almost like it's afraid to turn toward us and approach. I keep hoping that it will shift its head and look at us. We don't mean it any harm. I wave my arms.

"It's too far away to see you," Dale says.

"Let's paddle toward it," Burr says. He flings his arms in the water and begins to row. "Help me!"

I think about the sharks and I hesitate. But then Landon and Wick put their arms in the water too. I follow. We're turning the sea around the raft white, but we don't seem to be moving.

"Harder!" Burr yells.

But I'm already paddling as hard as I can.

"It's too far away," Sov says. "It's gone."

He's right. One by one, we pull our arms out of the water. There is a terrible silence broken only by the sound of droplets of seawater slipping off our skin and plinking into the raft's murky bottom. I try to offer reassurance. "If we came across one ship, we can come across another."

Burr stares in the direction of the ship, unbelieving.

I fold my arms across my chest. Darkness arrives unequivocally, like a train. The Sumatran rhino or boat or whatever it is continues to widen the horrible distance between us. To it, we are invisible.

"Stupid rhinoceros!" I yell.

Wick kisses my matted hair. "What are you talking about?" he asks.

"Why couldn't they see us?" I ask.

"They were just too far away," Wick says.

It's hard for me to accept that as the truth. But it must be true, because the gray block has disappeared. They've left us.

"The Coast Guard will come," Wick says. "We'll be okay."

A few stars pop on overhead, and a milky quarter moon glows in the distance. Sadly, there's just enough light so that I can make out what I think is a single circling fin. Or is it one of the ocean's many angular waves? The water tumbles upon itself. Small mountains of water rise and fall. I put my head down. I'm so thirsty.

"We should say a prayer," Burr says.

"Who should say it?" Landon asks.

"I could," Dale says.

I sense a potential argument. "Maybe we should each say our own silent prayer," I say.

"Good idea," Wick says.

We all bow our heads; even Skate dips his a bit lower.

"God, please send the Coast Guard—immediately. Amen," I say to myself.

I'm the first one to raise my head. I guess the others have longer requests.

Wick finishes too. He turns and reaches down, taking hold of my good hand. He gives it a squeeze and kisses my head again. Soon, everyone's head pops back up. Praying actually made me feel better. I'm a little surprised by how little effort it took to start relying on God.

"Hey, Enid. Do you want to know the fate of your shoe?" Munny turns to face me so he doesn't disturb Dale with more facts.

"Shark poop?" I ask.

"No, a shoe is indigestible," Munny says. "To get rid of

it, the shark will push its stomach out through its mouth. Once it gets the shoe out, the shark pulls its stomach back to where it belongs."

My mind draws a mental picture of what he's said, and I think of the shark vomiting up my mother's white pump by expelling its own stomach into the ocean. I wonder if that's what sharks do with bones. For them, are bones digestible or indigestible? I thank Munny for his information. But really, I wish he hadn't mentioned it. For the time being, I know all that I care to about sharks.

chapter 16

As night fully sets in, we start to doze. Skate has been sleeping for hours. Burr sits next to him, propping him up. Should I offer to do that? Do I have the strength? No.

"I'm going to rest," I say. I'm getting cold. I'm tired. Sleep feels better. It's okay if I sleep a little now. I rest my head in Wick's lap. He holds me by my shoulder and lightly rocks me. It's easy to drift off.

"Sweet dreams," he says.

I think I'm dreaming even as he says that. I feel like I'm at home. I see my room. I'm in it. Walking across the maple wood floors. My feet in socks. I am in two places at once. Here and there. As I zone out, I hear Wick and Landon speak in whispers. I think they are actually trying to have a conversation without my hearing them. Why? Why would they want to keep anything from me? Do they know something terrible that they don't want to tell me? I don't open my eyes. I listen.

"I'm trying to tell you that it's okay if Burr didn't call the Coast Guard, because she would have called the following day. Either way they're looking for us," Wick says.

"I don't know if that's true," Landon whispers.

"Yes," Wick says. "She'll know from the text. When

she showed up for breakfast she'd see the van, the empty boat slip, and put two and two together."

"You said nothing had been set in stone," Landon says.

"Right," Wick says. "But then I decided to invite her and I texted her. We used your phone, remember?"

Who are they talking about? Who did Wick text? I think back to the fact that the battery had died on his phone. Something is wrong. Is Wick seeing somebody? Was I right all along? I speak.

"Who are you talking about?"

"Nobody," Wick says. "Go back to sleep, Enid."

"I'm going to tell her," Landon says.

"She should know," Munny says from across the raft.

"What?" I ask.

"I'll tell her," Wick says. He traces his finger along my arm. "It doesn't mean anything. It's stupid. But after we decided to take a break, since I was going to be down here, I called Simone. We were supposed to meet for breakfast," Wick says.

Simone? Call? Breakfast?

"That's not the total truth," Sov says. "Tell her the total truth."

"Tell me," I say.

"We talked on the phone. We were going to hang out. We were just going to have fun together," Wick says.

"You came to Maryland to have fun with Simone," I say. "That's why you came."

"No," Wick protests. "I came for Burr and Skate and the last party before they head out to college. The Simone situation just happened."

I pull away from Wick. "No, the boat sinking just happened. The Simone thing was planned."

I try to stand. I feel so dizzy. The raft wobbles beneath my weight.

"Sit down!" Burr says.

I sit back down.

"What a mistake," Dale says. "You never should have told her."

"Shut up," I say. I hold my head. It's pounding.

"Wick, why don't you go sit next to Dale?" Landon says.

"Let's talk," Wick says, holding on to my leg.

"No!" I yell. "Let go of me."

He doesn't let go of me.

"I want to sit next to Munny and Sov," I say. I feel like I'm dying inside and out. As I leave my seat I tumble, and Landon catches me. "Were you going to tell me?" I ask. "Were any of you going to tell me?"

I take a seat on the other side of Munny.

"I thought about telling you when I found you in the bathroom," Sov says.

My mind sticks there. What if he had? Or what if I'd gotten off the boat before it had sailed? What if I'd made Landon come with me? What if I'd gotten so upset that I ruined the party and everyone got off the boat? I could have changed everything. We could be safe.

I hear myself scream. Skate lifts his head. "What? What? Enid are you okay?"

I look at Skate. He is wasting away. I can see the bones under his eyes. He looks like he's lost twenty pounds in two days.

"I'm okay," I say.

"You screamed," he says.

"She's a drama queen," Burr says.

I shake my head. "I am not."

"Your problems are nothing like mine. And do you hear me screaming?" Burr asks.

I think about his problems. He's an orphan. His twin is dying. And it's his fault we're all in this disaster. But I'm adrift at sea with a broken heart. All of our lives are terrible. Why am I still trying so hard to be right? Shouldn't I say something to make Burr feel better?

"You're right," I say. "I'm sorry."

To my surprise, Burr doesn't accept my apology. He doesn't say anything. He continues to hold his brother and glare into the sea. We drift. I listen to the small waves pushing us farther out to sea. They create a rhythm. My thoughts fall in sync with them. *Wick is a cheater. Wick lied. Wick is rotten. Get over him. Get over him.*

"I have something I need to say," Landon says.

I think it's going to be a condemnation of Wick. Because he should be condemned. I can't believe he was this dishonest.

"I never sent Simone that text message," Landon says.

"What do you mean? I was standing right there," Wick

says. "You're remembering things wrong."

"No, I remember," Landon says. "I wrote a text message. I typed what you told me to and I deleted it. I wasn't going to help you set up a date. I'm Enid's brother."

"Oh my God," Wick says.

"I know," Landon says.

"So she doesn't know. Because she didn't come. So she wouldn't have notified anybody," Wick says.

"Right," Landon says.

Burr never jumps in and claims that he called the Coast Guard. Why doesn't he? He just stares blankly into the distance.

"Burr, are you okay?" I ask.

He doesn't answer my question.

"I'm tired. I want to go to sleep," he says. He rests his head on the side of the raft.

It is stunning to think that Simone could have been responsible for my rescue. But she won't be. My hate for her begins to boil again.

"Enid," Wick says. "Are you okay?"

My hurt is exhausting me. I can't even answer him. As Burr sleeps, he stretches his legs out and they cross over mine. His jeans lift up and I can see his calves. They are covered in sores. I feel a hand on my own leg, and I jump. It's Munny.

"We can hope Burr called the Coast Guard," Munny says.

"Wouldn't they have been here by now?" Sov asks.

If Burr didn't, who would? The guys aren't expected

back for another day. And while I am officially missing, nobody knows where to look for me. Why didn't I leave a note with the marzipan? Why didn't I take the time to explain things to my mom and *then* abandon her?

The world feels so cold. But I won't give up. "Chances are we'll see another ship," I say. "This is the ocean. It's full of boats."

"It's full of sharks," Dale says.

"Don't say that," I plead. My world has been turned upside down, but I don't want to give up hope. "I feel like another ship is really close. We need to get some sleep. We can look for more boats in the morning."

"Yeah," Landon says. "That sounds good."

I wait for Sov and Munny to correct me and say that we're too far away from sailing routes to encounter more ships, but they don't. The silence bolsters me. It doesn't take me long to find the silver lining in Wick's betrayal. I have good instincts. Because if I was right about my Simone suspicions, I could be right about my boat suspicions. Even with a broken heart, I feel excited. As I let my head fall against my chest, there is a piece of me that looks forward to morning and what it might bring.

chapter 17

I'm in so much pain that my excitement fades quickly. The sores on my legs and arms have grown worse, and it makes it tougher to sleep. My lips are cracking. My tongue doesn't even feel like a tongue anymore. It's hard to sleep. Because my sadness nags at me. I drift off and wake up, feeling shattered.

Darkness lifts. This has been our second night in the water. The sun is starting to come up, casting a soft light on us. We are all exhausted. Everyone is sleeping except for me and Burr. It's Burr's turn to watch for the Coast Guard. Skate's condition is really weighing on him. I feel sorry for Burr, and I want to talk to him. I keep thinking back to what he said about his problems being worse than mine. I want to talk to him about this. Maybe if we talked he'd feel better. Wait. I shouldn't talk to him about his problems. What he needs is to start thinking about his future. Eager to cheer him, I launch ahead.

"College starts soon," I say.

Burr doesn't respond.

"Do you know where you'll be living on campus?" I ask.

"What?" He scowls at me.

"When you go to BYU," I say. "Is it set where you'll be

living?" I think this should buoy him, getting him to think about the stuff he has to look forward to.

"I don't want to talk about that," he says.

"When do—"

He cuts me off. "I don't want to talk at all."

"Okay," I say.

Burr is coming unglued. Landon says he drank more than anybody else. And after Skate, he looks the worst. His eyes are already sunken. I should give him what he wants. Silence. But it's hard to stay totally awake without conversation. I drift asleep. I'm not sure what wakes me. It might be the sound of water.

As I wake, I notice Burr leaning over the side of the raft. His back is to me, so I can't see exactly what he's doing. I think he's laughing. Wait. He's trying to block my view. I understand what's happening. Anger sweeps over me. I bet Burr has caught a fish. I bet Burr has caught a fish and he's not sharing it with anybody, not even Skate.

"Burr!" I scream. "Burr, what are you doing?"

Next to me, Landon jolts awake. "Do you see a ship?" he asks me.

"No, Burr is doing something. I think he's caught a fish."

Everybody is waking up now, even Skate. Burr slowly turns around to face me. His chin is glistening with water.

"Where did you get water?" Landon asks. "Do you have water?"

At first, Burr doesn't respond to Landon. He just smiles at us. I count as three tear-shaped drops bead onto his gray T-shirt. I can't believe he has water. I can't believe he wouldn't share.

"I've had it the whole time," Burr says.

His voice is wavering. He sounds like he's going to start laughing.

Dale lunges for Burr, and Wick has to hold him back by his pants.

"You make me sick," Dale yells. "We're dying. How can you hoard water from us? I bet he has the Doritos too."

Burr tilts his head up to the sky and howls. The sound is bone-chilling. He repeats it again and again. When he finally stops, Skate speaks.

"He's been giving me water," Skate says. "He hasn't been hoarding it."

This makes no sense to me. How can Burr have any water? Where did it come from? Then I notice his feet. He's put one shoe back on. The other is sitting next to him, filled to the brim with water.

"He's got water in his shoe," I say.

Dale lunges for it.

"Don't drink it!" Sov yells.

"Dude, I'm taking the first swig and then I'll pass it around."

He lifts the heel of the sneaker to his mouth and tips the water in. Immediately, he spits it out.

"It's salty," he says. "It's seawater."

Burr is laughing. "It's all mine. It's been here the whole time."

"Burr, you can't drink that," Wick says, fear in his voice. "It'll make you sicker."

Burr stands up. The raft sways unsteadily beneath his feet.

"It's made me feel so much better," Burr says. He howls again, and then sits down. "The bad water is on top, but if you reach down deep enough, it's good."

I close my eyes, but I can't fall asleep. This is too terrible. Why did Burr do this? Now he's going to die. And he's going to kill Skate too. I try to pretend none of this is true. I imagine our rescuers and what they're doing right now. They are in a ship looking for us. Talking about how we are like their own sons and daughters. They won't give up because people don't give up on their sons and daughters. I focus on my breathing. When I open my eyes, the Coast Guard might be here. A large white ship will be perched next to us, people waving at me from its bow, strong men tossing life preservers to us.

But I won't swim to them. Not with the sharks. They will have to come and get me. They will have to bring me to their ship and haul me aboard. When I step onto their deck, they'll give me water with large cubes of ice stacked in a glass like blocks. I'll drink it down and slide an ice cube into my mouth. My mouth will feel wet again. The Coast Guard will come, and they will give me everything I want.

"Coast Guard!" Burr yells. "Coast Guard!"

I open my eyes. I don't believe it. My dream has become my reality. The sun is a pink, happy color, staining the sky salmon. My heart is pounding.

"I don't see anything." My mouth is so dry that it's difficult to talk.

"There," Burr says. "It's right there."

We're all awake. But we're not searching the empty water. We're watching Burr.

"You should sit down," Dale says.

"Are you blind?" Burr says. "They're waving to us. Can't you see them?"

There is nothing there. The sharks don't even seem to be here this morning. The ocean is a blank slate.

"Get up and wave!" Burr shouts. "Let them know we see them."

I think about waving, but I don't. Why?

"The Coast Guard only comes once," Burr says.

Burr screams at the top of his lungs, waving his arms frantically. His desperation is palpable.

"Sov, give me your shirt," Burr says. "We need to flag it down. Yellow is the best color. Give me your life vest."

Sov looks to Munny. Munny shrugs. He hasn't spoken much after getting hit with the shoe. Now, a large purple crescent is forming below his left eye.

"Sov, I need the shirt," Burr says. "Give it."

Sov shakes his head.

"I don't see anything," Sov says. "I don't see the Coast Guard."

"Shit, you guys!" Burr says. "I'm the captain. It's my job to save you. I called the Coast Guard, and here they are."

"Dude, sit here," Dale says, patting an empty spot on the raft next to him.

Burr looks at Dale and balls his hands into fists.

"There's nothing there," Landon says. "You're seeing things. It's the effects of dehydration."

Munny and Sov both nod enthusiastically.

"I guess I'm gonna have to swim to them and bring the Coast Guard right to your sorry asses," Burr says.

Skate grabs the cuff of Burr's jeans.

"Don't go," Skate says.

"I gotta save us," Burr says.

I don't believe that he's going to jump. I don't think any of us does. But he jumps. He splashes into the ocean wearing all of his clothes and that stupid shoe, and starts swimming away from the raft toward absolutely nothing. I watch his blond head as he turns it from side to side to breathe in air. His arms take long strokes, and his feet stir the water as he kicks himself forward.

"Get back in the raft!" Dale yells. He's got his arm stretched out toward Burr.

"Come back!" Skate yells. "Don't leave."

I'm in shock. I watch Burr moving farther away from the raft. His swimming body ripples the calm water.

"Should I go after him?" Landon asks me.

"Burr, bring your ass back here right now!" Dale yells.

"I don't know what you should do," I say.

Skate sits straight up, and Wick and Landon move to his side.

"I gotta help him," Skate says.

Skate is covered in sores, and his head wound is so infected that I think he might have blood poisoning.

"You can't help him," Wick says. His face looks desperate. He puts his arm around Skate. "He's gone."

Munny, Sov, and Dale dip their arms into the water up to their shoulders, and try to paddle the raft toward Burr. Landon and Wick do the same, but as they keep paddling, they struggle to row the ship forward. I reach an arm in too. The water feels frigid. Using all my energy, I claw at the sea.

Burr howls. He sounds happy, like he's enjoying himself. But then the sound abruptly ends, in mid-howl, and there is silence. I think I hear a splash. Skate grabs his legs and screams in pain. We keep paddling. *Faster. Faster.*

"Help him," Skate cries. Skate gasps several times. "He can't breathe."

In the distance, I think I can see the color red blooming in the water. I don't hear any cries. Burr must be underwater. A shark is eating him beneath the surface. I don't see a frenzy of sharks. I stop paddling and bring my arm back into the raft. We all watch the spot for a long moment. Eventually, one lone dorsal fin, missing a chunk of its skin, slides up out of the water and glides away. Then nothing. Everyone else draws their arms out of the water. To dry them off, they shake them hard, and several clean beads of water slide across my legs. If it were warm, the sun would evaporate them. But it's not warm. I shiver.

Other than the water-filled sneaker that he left behind, it's as if Burr were never here at all. We sit in this awful silence. How can any of us ever feel anything close to happiness again? The seconds tick by. They turn into minutes. After about an hour it's time for somebody to speak. I hear my own voice. I say what we're all thinking.

"Burr never called the Coast Guard," I say. "I don't think anyone is coming for us."

I turn and look back at the spot where Burr went down. There's nothing there. Burr Riggs doesn't exist anymore. Sure, his spirit might be weaving through the heavens, but that's not the same thing. He's gone. Forever.

I put my head in my hands. I can't believe our ship sank. I can't believe that I just saw my friend get eaten by a shark. Life is not fair. This world will swallow anyone. Even if you know how to swim.

I keep drifting off. Every time I open my eyes, I expect to see Burr. Because what happened can't have really happened. I look at Skate. He doesn't talk. I can see the skeleton of his face beneath his skin. His cheeks have caved in. He moans when he sleeps. I don't know what to do. Dale sits next to him. He's taken his Windbreaker off and created a tent of shade over Skate's upper body. Dale tells him jokes. They're mostly dirty. I can't always hear the punch lines. I didn't realize Dale had this much empathy inside of him.

Wick keeps looking at me. He's across the raft from me. He has tried to reach out and touch me. He wants to make up. "How are you feeling?" he asks.

"Leave me alone," I say.

"Enid, what if one of us dies? Is this how you want it to end?" Wick asks.

"Don't do that," Landon says. "Don't put it to her like that."

"Fine," Wick says. But he's still looking at me.

Landon sits next to me. My head feels so heavy, I lean it on his shoulder.

"Ouch. You're stabbing me with your barrette," he says.

I sit back up. I don't want to stab my brother.

"Do you want me to take your barrette out? It's all caught up in your hair. Does it hurt?"

He tugs at the silver barrette. But I don't want him to take it out. On this raft, it's one of the few things that I can call mine.

"No," I say. "I want to keep it."

"Hey," Munny says. "Maybe we could use that to make a fishing lure."

"Good idea," Sov says.

"My barrette?" I ask. I don't want to lose it. I don't want to drop it into the sea.

"That could work," Wick says.

"Do you still have the cash rope we made out of the twenties?" Landon asks.

"We could bend the fastener to make a hook," Munny says.

Skate moans. I don't think it's related to our conversation.

"No," I say.

"No?" Landon asks.

"That would never work," I say.

"It might," Munny says.

"No!" I try to think of a reason to keep it that doesn't make me sound self-centered or unreasonable. "We could use it to signal a boat or a plane. It's metal. It's shiny."

"I guess," Dale says. "But we could use it right now to find food."

I shake my head.

"Okay," Wick says. "Let her keep it."

I wish Landon would stick up for me instead of Wick. I don't want Wick to be on my side anymore.

We stop debating my barrette. We drift. I think about what Wick said. Is this how I want things to end between us? What if he *did* die? What if *I* die? I am staring at him. He is staring at me.

"What are you thinking?" Wick asks.

"You lied," I say.

"Not totally. I didn't know whether or not I would call her until after we decided to take a break," Wick says.

I don't believe him. It doesn't matter.

"Don't think about that," Landon says. "Focus on your glaciers."

"Glaciers?" I ask. I don't know what he's talking about.

"Your life-sustaining wish," Landon says.

My life-sustaining wish? My slow mind finally finds it.

"That was a dumb choice. I should have said Machu Picchu. I've always wanted to go to Peru," I say.

"Do both," Landon says.

"Yeah," I say. I am tired of sitting up. I lean into the side of the raft and look over into the water. The water is very clear and blue. It's gorgeous. "The ocean looks different."

"We're in the Gulf Stream," Munny says. "That's why it's so blue."

"What does that mean?" I ask.

"It means we're drifting toward the Arctic Sea," Munny says.

"You mean, that's one possibility," I say. "We could be drifting toward land, right?"

"No, we're drifting farther out. And north," Munny says.

"I think he's right," Wick says.

"Dude, it's time we call a spade a shovel. We're all gonna die," Dale says.

Skate moans loudly, and the conversation stops. Dale lowers his jacket and drapes it across Skate's chest. After a long silence, Munny speaks.

"We could always come across a fishing ship," he says.

"What are the odds that's gonna happen? Like one in a billion?" Dale says.

Wick leans across the raft and shoves Dale in his chest. "Let up," Wick says. "Think about Mom and Dad. It will kill them if we don't make it back. You want to talk about odds. What are the odds that our boat would sink and we'd end up in this raft and still be alive?"

Wick's words silence everyone. I search their faces. I think we all start concentrating on our families. I imagine my mother. She stands in the kitchen, her brown hair pulled into a low ponytail, her green eyes lined with a light charcoal color. She's baking a wedding cake. The timer on the stove top dings. Using her mitted hands, she pulls a large circle pan from the oven. The batter has turned a golden color, and the cake top has risen to form a perfectly even dome.

Her breath mixes with the oven's heat, and a pillow of steam forms in front of her face. She closes her eyes and inhales. She sets it on a wire rack on our kitchen counter. My mother loves weddings: the happy brides and anxious grooms. I think she misses the romance that somehow drained out of her own life. I can smell the scent of vanilla wafting off of the hot pans. Then I conjure up my father's face as he walked down the stairs to his new lair. I stay in the kitchen with my mother, and then I slink away. Though it comforts me that he's inside this daydream, I don't want to spend any time with him.

Noon arrives. The bright sun is directly overhead. We've been adrift for a day and a half, and the raft continues to grow a crust of salt. It looks like lace. Or snow. But it's salt. The waves have remained calm ever since the big storm. I wish it would rain. I'm dying to have some moisture to dampen my tongue and the inside of my cheeks. If I had enough liquid in me to pee, I think I would drink my own urine. I can't believe I'm thinking this way. I'd do anything for a taste of something wet.

The sun is heating the water that's gathered at the bottom of the boat. It's releasing a thick, disgusting smell.

"We should dump the raft out and get rid of this crap," Dale says. He kicks at the water with his shoe, accidentally splashing some on Skate.

Skate moans.

"This crap is giving me sores," Dale says. He lifts up his pant leg and reveals several oval, festering patches.

"We all have those," I say. "It's from the exposure."

"She's right," Munny says.

"The sludge in the raft can't be helping. It's gonna make us sick," Dale says.

A part of me knows that he's right, but really, there's nothing we can do.

"Let's use a shoe and bail out the water," Wick says.

It's a good idea. I'm surprised none of us thought of that. I guess that we're so worn down that both our minds and our bodies are weak.

Skate is holding Burr's sneaker to his chest.

Wick sorts through the pile to find his own sneaker and begins bailing out the water. Landon follows suit and joins in. My hand is so raw and puffy that I can't make myself touch the water. After emptying their shoes out several times, they stop.

"We've got out as much as we can," Wick says.

"Let me see that," Dale says. He grabs Landon's shoe, and scoops at the inch of contaminated water still left in the raft. But Dale can't position the shoe in a way to drain any more. He jams the shoe at the floor, and eventually flings it into the sea.

"That was so stupid of you," Landon says. "Think before you pull that crap."

"Shut up," Dale says. "Once we're dead, we're not going to need our shoes anyway."

Wick glares at Dale.

"You need to grow up," Wick says. "And fast."

"What you did with that shoe, that's a $25,000 fine," I say.

"You did the same damn thing with your own shoe," Dale says.

"But you've done it twice," I say.

"Knock it off," Wick says.

Wick shouldn't be telling me what to do. I turn and look out into the water. And when I do, I am shocked by what I see. It's awful. One more new thing that could kill us.

"Eel!" I yell. "Eel!" I point into the water.

Everybody stares.

"What is it?" Landon asks.

I know what it is. I can tell by its outline. "It's a giant eel!"

"Can we eat it?" Dale asks.

"Eels live in reefs," Munny says. "I don't think it's an eel."

"But if it is an eel, we can eat it, right?" Dale asks.

Munny doesn't answer him. Nobody seems nervous that it's headed right toward the raft.

"That's definitely not a giant eel," Munny says.

But I know what I'm seeing. It's long and dark and the top of its head bobs in the water as it climbs over tiny white-tipped waves to reach us.

"Wait. It's not even a fish, is it?" Dale asks.

We're nervous as we search the water. We don't want anything else attacking us.

"It looks like an alligator," Dale says.

Is that even possible?

"It's brown," I say, as if a color-identification is useful.

"It looks like a log," Landon says.

"A log?" I ask. Why would we come across a log? I lift my hand to my forehead. It does look like a log. I become filled with hope. "This is great! It means we're close to land, right?"

"We're not close to land," Munny says. "We're drifting farther out."

We're looking at a log. A log used to be a tree. Trees grow on land. We want to reach land. I'm confused.

"Munny's right," Wick says.

I try to stand, to get a better view of the log. My movement jostles Skate, and he releases a soft groan.

"Sit down," Dale says.

I sit. "If we're drifting farther out, how did we find a tree?"

"It's drifting too," Sov says.

"Ever heard of driftwood?" Skate asks.

I'm surprised that he's coherent. I'm shocked he's forming words.

"I have," I say.

"Stupid dick log," Dale says.

"It's better than a killer eel," I say.

"I never thought it was an eel," Dale says.

I hold my head in my hands. I want off the raft. I want out of this sea existence. I try to force a daydream to come.

"Wait. Maybe it's not a stupid dick log. Do you think we could break it apart and make paddles?" Dale asks.

"I don't know," Wick says. "Maybe."

"Let's get it!" Dale says.

I haven't seen him this excited since he got that gymnast's phone number.

"It's too far away," Munny says. "It has to drift closer."

It is drifting closer. Soon, it's only as far away as a car.

"Reach for it," Dale says.

He's stretching his arms into the water, but he's not even close to making contact.

"Hold me. I'm going to use my legs," he says.

Wick takes hold of Dale's arms as he sits on the edge and fully extends his legs in the water. I worry that a shark might come and bite them off. Nobody else mentions this possibility. The log inches closer. Dale touches it with his socked foot. It bobs away.

"Come here!" Dale says.

"You're getting it," Landon says.

Dale tries again. This time he's able to apply pressure and the log moves much closer toward us. Landon is able to reach out and take hold of the damp wood.

"We did it!" Dale says.

Wick yanks on him and pulls him back into the raft. Landon slaps at the wet log, trying to break a piece of it off.

"It's solid," Landon said. "No way we're breaking it apart."

"Let me try," Wick says. He begins to move toward our side of the raft.

"Wait," Landon said. "We need to watch how we distribute the weight."

Wick stops. Dale sits down next to Skate. He's exhausted.

"Let's break it apart later," Dale says.

"There's no way," Landon says.

It must be very solid. Because Landon doesn't register even the slightest bit of hope.

"We should keep it," Dale says.

"Why?" I ask.

I watch Landon strain to keep hold of it beside the raft.

"If something happens and we have to abandon the raft, we can use it to float," Dale says.

"What about the sharks?" I ask.

"We might need the log," Dale says.

It makes no sense. "Don't wear yourself out trying to hold onto it," I tell Landon.

His hand is placed firmly on the log. As it bobs, Landon's hand keeps getting submerged in the water. That has to hurt. Our flesh is rotting even without being in the water.

"Maybe we could use it," Landon says. "I'm good for now."

"We should trade soon," I say. "Landon shouldn't have to hold it the whole time."

"I'll take it next," Dale says.

We drift. The sun pounds us. Nobody is talking. Skate isn't moaning. The foreverness of the ocean feels so grim.

There's a splash. On Dale's side of the raft, a shark bumps the raft hard.

"Christ!" Dale says. Like a protector, he throws an arm over Skate. We all look into the water. The shark doesn't look familiar to me. I haven't seen Belly or Chip for hours. I refuse to think about the last time I saw Notch. I think Notch is an evil fish. It doesn't have a heart. Or a soul. It's just a blob of cartilage. An evolutionary mistake. A mouth. I close my eyes. And we continue to drift. And drift. And drift.

chapter 19

I sleep and I sleep and I sleep. Why? For the sake of dreams. To push away my hunger and my thirst. Because as my body creeps closer to exhaustion and death, my hope, my light, my soul shrinks. It's late afternoon. My sleep is broken when I hear Munny's voice.

He leans over and whispers in my ear, "I think Skate is dying."

This news makes me feel like a person again. I'm alert. I have something to tend to. I look to Skate. His eyes are sunken. His body is covered in sores, and he's running a high fever. I feel helpless. I don't think that there is anything any of us can do.

"How are you feeling, Skate?" I ask. My voice is raspy; it's painful to talk.

Skate's eyes flutter and open. "Is Burr back yet?" he asks.

Skate holds his brother's shoe on his chest. He's delirious. He's forgotten that Burr is never coming back. Do I tell him his brother is dead? Do I lie to him? I'm sixteen. How am I supposed to know what to do? I've had my driver's license for less than a year. I struggle with trigonometry. Issues concerning death are beyond me. I think of the monogrammed towel in the bathroom. The

Riggses. They are gone. Burr is gone. Skate is barely here.

Dale stays on one side of Skate, and I move to the other side.

"He's not back yet," I say.

"My mom bought us these for college. They're weather-proof," he says. "Good in snow. Good in heat. Utah has both."

He's talking about the shoe. His hands look so white holding it, like there isn't any blood in them. I smile down at him. The shoe is a soggy, ruined leather mess. "They look real nice," I say.

"If I fall asleep, when he comes back, will you wake me?" he asks.

"Sure," I say.

Skate doesn't respond. I can't tell if he's passed out or asleep.

"We shouldn't lie to him," Dale says.

I glance at him. He's far gone, making the tent shade with his Windbreaker for Skate. Dale looks ready to put it on again. "Everything is okay," I tell Skate.

"I know you don't believe that," Dale says. Should I be telling Skate the truth? Am I making things worse by trying to make things sound okay?

"I'm doing my best," I say. "I never imagined I'd be adrift on a ship with a bunch of guys in the middle of the Atlantic. I'm doing my best."

"This is a raft, not a ship," says Dale. "The ship sank."

The sound Skate makes as he breathes doesn't remind me of breathing at all. It's like air is escaping out of him.

Dale isn't looking at Skate. He's watching the water.

"How is the log?" Dale asks Landon. "Do you want me to hold it?"

How can he even be thinking about the log? "Yeah," Landon says. "Your turn."

Dale and Landon change places. Skate moans a little as the raft shifts beneath him. "It's okay," I say. I lean back. I close my eyes. I listen to the water. It ripples and ripples and ripples.

At the sound of Skate's voice, I wake up. It sounds happy, and I have no idea why. It's twilight. I imagine that the sharks have returned. It's the beginning of our third night in the water.

"I've been waiting for you," Skate says. He's speaking to the air in front of him. He lifts the shoe up. "I got it." Skate happily nods his head. His neck looks so thin. "Yeah," he says. His voice is growing softer. "I'm ready." I realize that his eyes are closed.

"Skate, buddy, are you okay?" Dale asks.

We're all staring at Skate. We want him to open his eyes and tell us that he's been dreaming. Skate rests his head back into the raft's side. We've been adrift for over forty-eight hours, and the inflated walls have softened. Skate's lips are still moving, but we can't hear him. I lean in very close to him. I don't talk to him. I don't want to interrupt whatever is happening.

"Enid," he whispers to me.

I'm surprised that he knows that I'm next to him. I thought he was totally out of it.

"I think I'm gonna go," he says.

I remember Burr jumping overboard, and I don't want Skate to do that.

"No," I say. "You're safe in the raft."

"I know," he says. He's speaking so softly that I have to lower my ear to his cracked lips. His breathing is shallow. Even though my face is right next to his mouth, I can barely feel air touch my cheek. "I miss Burr. I miss my family."

I squeeze his hand. "I know you do," I say. "I miss him too. We all do."

There's a pause.

"I think I'm gonna go," he says.

My throat constricts. I am shattered. I think I can feel my heart. Inside of me, everything feels hot with pain. "No, try to stay."

Nobody else says anything. They're letting me do all the talking.

"No," he says. "I can't stay."

I take his hand and squeeze it. I'm so tired. I don't know what I'm supposed to tell him.

"Okay," I say. "If that's what you want. You should go."

His lips curl into a smile. He exhales several small breaths. "Thanks, Enid."

His fever is so high, I feel like I'm sitting next to a space heater. He struggles to inhale a few more times. His breathing is shallow. Then, I feel one long breath warm my cheek. Skate's fingers loosen around my hand. I let go of him. I look at him. His eyes are closed. He's still clutching Burr's shoe.

"Is he gone?" Munny asks.

I nod my head.

"What should we do?" Wick asks.

Nobody answers. We drift for what feels like an hour, but it's probably only a few minutes.

"We shouldn't keep his body in the boat," Munny says.

I can't imagine getting rid of Skate. He is our friend.

"Let's just sit here for a minute," Dale says. "I'm not ready to do that."

We drift. The raft feels so quiet.

"I need to say something," Munny says. "But I don't want anybody to get upset."

I have no idea what Munny is going to say.

"We won't get upset," Wick says.

"When people get lost at sea, they've been known to eat whatever meat they can to survive," he says.

"You think we should eat Skate?" Landon asks.

"Turn into cannibals?" Wick adds.

"I'm not saying I want to do it," Munny says. "I'm just saying it's something that's been done before."

"There's no way," Landon says. "We're not eating Skate."

"You're right," Munny says. "I don't think we should do it."

"You are crazy," Dale says. "Nobody eats their friends. What's wrong with you? I know what's wrong with you.

You're saying this shit because that's the kind of people you come from."

"Wait. I don't want to eat Skate," Sov says. "I think it's a bad idea."

"I thought I should bring it up," Munny says. "It's happened."

Dale is so frustrated he looks like a different person. His face is wrinkled and upset. "It has never happened, Munny, that a group of friends go sailing and their boat sinks and some of them die. Some of the unlucky bastards cease to be, and then their friends eat them. Never," Dale says.

Munny continues. "I've read about it happening with whaling ships. Some of the crew of the whaleship *Essex*, a Nantucket ship, ate crew members, because there was nothing else. If they hadn't, they all would've died. I'm thinking about all of us and our survival."

"Dude, I'd eat the damn raft before I'd eat Skate," Dale says. "Besides, nobody's even heard of the whaleship *Essex*. Your fact box is broken. I think you're making it up."

"Herman Melville had heard of it. *Moby-Dick* is based on the *Essex*," Munny said.

"No!" Landon says. "Stop! No more fighting. This is stupid. Look. Look at what's happening to us."

We all stare at Landon. He sounds so certain.

"Skate's body can't stay in the raft," Landon says.

"I agree," Sov says.

"Yeah," Munny says.

"I guess we have to do it," Wick says.

"We just dump him?" I ask.

Landon nods. I cannot believe this.

"Okay," I say. But I don't know if it is okay.

"Wait," Dale says. "Could you hold the log for me?"

Wick agrees and extends his arms out, gripping the enormous piece of driftwood at one end. Dale digs in his pocket. He pulls out the pale pink pebble. "It's from the cemetery. I picked it up after the funeral, right after the Riggses were buried. It got stuck in my shoe." He stares at the small rock. "I'm not sure what I was saving it for. But I think it should go with him."

We silently watch as Dale takes the pebble and slides it into Skate's front pocket.

Even though we've all agreed that Skate needs to be taken off the raft, at least five minutes have passed and we're still staring at his body.

"It's time to take him off the boat," Landon says.

"We're going to have to lift him into the water," Wick says.

"Dude!" Dale hollers. He stands up, which surprises me, because I don't think I'd have the strength to do that. He locks his knees and his legs wobble. "We're on a freaking raft, not a boat!" Then he sits down.

We're all so tired. I look at Skate's body, then I close my eyes.

"We've been at sea for two days," Landon says. "We need some rules."

I'm surprised to hear Landon saying this. Up to now

in life, he's been a pretty much a follower.

These are Landon's rules:

Rule one: It's okay to call the raft a ship.

Rule two: We are all family on this ship.

Rule three: You can never drink the ocean.

Rule four: If you die, we'll roll your body into the sea.

I'm happy that he stopped at four rules, because I don't think I'd be able to keep any more than that in my head. I'm relieved. I like the rules. When Landon's finished explaining the rules, Wick asks Munny to hold the log. I think we should release it. We're wasting so much of our energy. But I don't want to start a fight. That wastes energy too. Landon, Wick, and Dale carefully lift Skate into the ocean. They treat him like an extremely fragile package, like he's made entirely of glass. Skate's body slips in and floats facedown. Now in the water, the dried blood from his wound begins to dissolve, and his blond hair splays like a fan.

Dale takes the log.

"We should all close our eyes," Munny says.

"Why?" I ask. For me, it's sad but comforting to watch Skate peacefully drift away. Then I spot the dark fins. I shut my eyes. I hear the sound of splashing. I feel water being sloshed into the raft. I feel the raft being jerked and bumped. One shark must be feeding on Skate from beneath the raft. I can feel it under us. It's big and strong and pushes the raft dangerously close to tipping several times. I lower myself to the raft's floor and kneel. I can feel the shark's body moving powerfully beneath my legs.

Only rubber separates us. He slams against my shins.

"I'm losing the log!" Dale says.

I hope he does. Landon puts his arm around me.

"We're gonna be okay," he says. "I can feel it."

I decide not to feel anything. I make my mind, my body, everything go blank. Then the shark beneath the raft rams us hard, trying—I believe—to make us flip. When it does this, I realize that I hate the shark. If I had a gun, I would aim it at that fish and sink bullet after bullet into its lousy gray head. I totally understand why they blew up Jaws at the end of the movie. If I had explosives, I'd reduce each shark out here to liquid and guts. God, I really hate them all. Then, I have my own small epiphany: I hate these sharks because I want to live. And I'm glad to know this.

When I open my eyes I see a red drop of water running down my thigh. I wipe it off with my good hand. I rub and rub until the skin on my leg is absolutely dry. I bring my fingers to my lips and kiss my hand. Then I press it against my heart.

I close my eyes again. Six out of eight, I wonder. That's possible. Six out of eight can survive, right? I'm not asking for the impossible, am I?

chapter 20

It's dark and frigid, much colder than last night. My teeth chatter as Landon and Wick huddle over me.

"Sov, Munny, join us," Landon says.

"Dale, come over," Wick says. "Cuddle up. It'll be warmer."

"No. We need to keep the raft balanced," Munny says.

"We should huddle three and three," Landon says. "Dale, join them."

"No," Munny says.

"What do you mean, no?" Landon asks. "Do it to survive."

"Not with Dale," Munny says.

"I'm not a big fan of yours either," Dale says.

"Come on," Landon says. "Remember rule number two: We are family on this ship. Families suck it up and stick together. Families huddle for warmth."

My head is down. The bodies hovering over me block the wind. I can't see Munny's face. I can't tell what the problem is.

"Dale is an ignorant racist, and I refuse to huddle with him," Munny says.

"Me too," Sov says.

"I don't even know what you're talking about," Dale says.

A cold wind blows against my right cheek. Landon and Wick both sit upright, taking away my wind barrier.

"What are you talking about?" Wick asks.

"Ask your brother what he meant when he said that me and Sov wanted to eat Skate because that's the kind of people we were, the kind of people we came from?"

"He didn't mean anything by that," Wick says. "He says stupid crap all the time."

"Hey," Dale says. "Watch the insults."

"He's a racist," Munny says, "and he knows it."

Nobody is in the huddle anymore, and the wind is smacking my neck and face and tunneling into my ears.

"Maybe I did mean something by it," Dale said. "So what? I apologize."

"Nice apology," Sov mumbles.

"We need to stick together," Landon says. "Come on."

"Dale, what kind of people do you think I come from?" Munny asks.

"I know I've made mistakes. You think I don't know that? You think I don't know when I'm acting and not acting like an asshole?" Dale asks.

"Yes," Munny says.

They should stop fighting. I don't think they're accomplishing anything. But then, what did Dale mean by that comment? When he said it, it went over my head.

"What did you mean by it?" I ask.

"They're Cambodians. I read that they eat their own dogs there and stuff."

"Where did you read that?" Munny asks.

Dale shrugs. "I guess I heard it. I had a third cousin who fought in Vietnam. At a barbecue I heard him talk about how sometimes people ate other people's dogs."

"You're an idiot. Don't ever talk to me again," Munny says.

I don't know whether it matters that people eat dogs during a crisis. I say something to try to buffer the tension. "Didn't Lewis and Clark eat dogs when they were exploring and ran out of normal food?" I ask.

"Isn't there a country that eats black dogs in winter?" Wick asks.

"Is it Cambodia?" Dale asks.

"Shut up," Munny says. "You don't know geography. You don't know history. You don't know anything. For instance, Cambodia and Vietnam are separate countries."

"But they touch each other," Dale says.

"You suck," Sov says.

"Do you separate the U.S. from Canada? Or Mexico? Or is that all the same to you, too?" Munny asks.

"That's totally different."

"Only to you, Dale. You are such an ignorant racist," Munny says.

"Don't call me that. I was guessing at which countries eat dogs," Dale says.

I'm not surprised that Munny is so bothered about this. But I don't think it helps him to get this upset. He shouldn't waste his energy on Dale.

"Be mad at him later. Focus on yourself," I tell Munny.

"Right," Munny says.

This isn't like Munny at all. He's usually pretty mellow. I guess everybody has a limit. Dale sits still. I sort of expect him to lunge at Munny or flip him off. But he doesn't. He probably doesn't want to let go of his precious log. I close my eyes. I wish there were a way to close my ears.

Dale makes sounds like he's close to crying.

"You've never asked me anything about Cambodia," Munny says.

"Or Ireland," Sov says.

"So you know, our grandparents died in the Killing Fields. Our mom barely escaped," Munny says.

I'm surprised that Munny's mouth is making enough spit for him to utter all these syllables. I couldn't.

"Don't you have anything to say now?" Munny asks.

Dale doesn't respond. I bet he feels like a huge jerk. I feel a little bit like that, and I'm not even involved with the fight.

"Calm down," Landon says. "You've made your point."

"He didn't mean it," Wick says. "He's always saying stuff that he doesn't mean."

My head rests against Landon. When he speaks, I can hear the sound coming from deep inside of him. I listen to his heartbeat. I think about how at one point the two of us were both curled up inside my mother's womb. I don't know if it's normal to think about the start of your life during times like this or not. I guess it makes sense. This could be the end.

chapter 21

We drift and we drift. When I close my eyes, I'm back in Vermont. Back in Burlington. I'm walking down Church Street. Bells jingle when I walk into Ben & Jerry's and buy a Cherry Garcia milkshake. The boy working the counter tells me it's my lucky day. He says that all the milkshakes are bottomless, and he pours me another one. When I open my eyes, I'm sucking on my bottom lip, and my head is tucked into Landon's smelly armpit.

"Do I stink too?" I ask.

"Yeah," Landon says.

"As bad as you?"

"No, you still smell a little bit like a girl," he says.

A dull light washes over us. It must be close to morning. Looking around, I realize now that one side of the raft is too empty. With Dale still trying to hold onto his log and Wick switching turns with him, and everybody else avoiding the spots left by Skate and Burr, we're not doing a good enough job balancing the raft.

"Someone should sit there," I say.

Munny and Sov look at each other. Wick leans forward and begins to crawl toward the spot.

"No, I'll go," I say. "I could use the change of scenery."

Landon squeezes my hand and then lets go. I inch my way to my new spot. I lean my head back a bit. My neck feels tired. I'm surprised that I never noticed how heavy my head was until now. I heard somewhere that the human head weighs ten pounds. Mine feels like it's pushing thirty. I close my eyes. I feel somebody touching my leg, and I open my eyes and see Dale. I flinch.

"No, don't," he says. "I want you to know that I'm sorry about what I said."

I nod. He's said so many rude, offensive, and ridiculous things that I'm not even sure what he's referring to.

"About your cut and leaving a blood trail," he adds.

"Oh, okay," I say. Maybe he thinks he's going to die, and he needs to confess his sins. To be honest, I feel like confessing a few things too. Something about impending death makes you want to lighten your soul.

He turns to Sov and Munny.

"Dudes, I'm sorry about what I said about Cambodia. And I'm sorry about your grandparents."

I search Dale's sunburned face. He looks sincere about this.

Munny and Sov don't respond. They're much more stoic than I am.

"Did you ever meet them?" Dale asks.

"They were killed before we were born," Sov says. "My mother was only five."

"Yeah, she escaped into to Thailand and then made it to California with a group of refugees," Munny says.

"I'm sorry," Dale says.

We drift for a moment in silence, but then Dale speaks again.

"Can I ask you two something?"

Sov and Munny shrug their shoulders.

"So, what do your names mean?"

"Sov means Saturday, and Munny means wise," Munny answers. "They're traditional Cambodian names."

"Oh, that's cool. I'm named after an uncle who was a coal miner. He died in an explosion when he was really young. Twenty."

"I didn't know that," I say. That means Wick's uncle was killed in a mine explosion. I wonder why he never told me this. I glance at him. Our eyes lock, but neither of us says anything. I break his gaze and look back to Sov and Munny and Dale. All this time I've been so focused on the current tragedy.

"You are going to kiss Dina Sneed. You are going to start a blog." I point at Munny and Sov as I remind them of their wishes. "I am going to Machu Picchu." After aiming my finger at myself I direct it toward Dale. "And you are going to toot some blow."

Dale's mouth turns into a smile, stretching the skin, popping the scabs on his lips open. "Maybe I should skip the cocaine and go to Machu Picchu too."

I'm sure he's kidding around, but his answer surprises me.

"Not with me," I say, joking and not joking at the same time.

"I bet you change your mind," he says. "I've got

good endurance. I'd carry the tent."

I don't think hiking Machu Picchu works that way. I think you have to go with an official tour group, and they provide the tents. But I don't tell Dale this. I only manage to say, "Hmm."

"I could hike the shit out of that mountain," Dale assures me. He rubs at the broken scabs on his lips, smearing blood on his fingers and mouth.

Does he really want me to agree to let him join me on my life-sustaining wish? I am too tired to consider hiking a mountain with Dale.

"I'll carry the water too," he says.

I consider this. "We're going to need a ton."

"As much as you want," Dale says.

I can't believe I'm going along with this.

"I'll come too," Landon says.

"Yeah," Munny says. "I like to hike."

"Don't leave me out," Sov says.

I like that my wish is becoming a group goal.

"I won't leave you out," I say. I know what that feels like.

"Am I invited?" Wick asks.

I don't answer him right away. The time that I don't speak stretches on for painful seconds. I imagine Machu Picchu in my mind. I've only seen pictures of the Inca foot trail a couple of times. A rocky green mountain juts out of a tropical forest. And the ruins of the ancient city are spread over hills. Stone walls. Main squares. Temples. Palaces. Stairways. Fountains. I focus so hard it's as if the photograph is inside me. "Machu Picchu," I mumble. I don't really want him to come with us. Nobody says anything.

"Can I come?" Wick asks again.

I shake my head, but I don't say no. "We'll see," I finally say. I close my eyes and the guys keep talking. About Cambodia? Machu Picchu? Cocaine? I'm not sure. I keep imagining the Inca ruins. I have a backpack. I have my friends. *Everybody needs to move closer together so I can get more of the mountain behind you*, I tell them. I lift my camera and take a picture of everything. *Click*. And I quickly drift off.

chapter 22

We're sunburned. We're dehydrated. We're starving. We're screwed. It's noon again. The sun is directly overhead, and this is our third day in the water. Sov and Munny said that a person could go without water for three days in these conditions. This is it. I honestly believe that at any moment I could die. Any of us could die. I mean, it's already happened twice.

My legs are flung out in front of me. It hurts to bend them. They don't look like my legs anymore either. They resemble something you'd read about in a medical textbook in a chapter dedicated to gross diseases that rot away lower extremities. I bet dead people's legs look better than mine. I'm so tired.

I lean my head back on the raft's softening side. I know this is dangerous. A shark could come along and bite my head right off. Sov and Munny have warned us that sharks are capable of jumping directly into the raft. They say that they've read about that sort of thing happening to sailors in open boats. I never realized that sharks could propel themselves out of the water high enough to do that. But I bet they can. From what I've seen thus far, they're crazy powerful beasts.

After this, I swear I'll never go in the water again. No

lakes, no rivers, no streams, no canals, no swamps, no oceans, no puddles, no ponds, and no Jacuzzis. I don't even want to see a camel and its water-filled humps. They are all dead to me. I'm even going to quit the swim team. I doubt I'll even take baths. I'll be one of those people who only showers. When the time comes, I won't even need to buy a home with a tub.

Once I get out of here, I'm never going to read a thing more about sharks or the sea either. I'm never even going to watch films that feature it, not even the movie *Titanic*, which was a pretty good film. None of the people who were on that ship had to worry about sharks. Their biggest hurdle was the cold. I'd rather face the cold than sharks any day of the week. But I guess if I were facing freezing temperatures, by day three I'd already be dead. Though I bet freezing to death isn't as bad as this. I think about asking Landon which he thinks is worse, freezing to death or being eaten by sharks. But I don't. I sense he's in a hopeful mood, and I don't want to spoil it.

I'm totally awake, but I keep my eyes closed. It's so hard to look at myself or anyone else. And I don't really want to see Wick anyway. I don't have the energy to wonder about what's going to happen to us. Every few minutes, Landon touches my calf. He reaches down with his pointer finger and traces the letters *E C C*. They're my initials. I think he's trying to remind me that I'm a person. That I have a life. That I shouldn't throw in the towel. Speaking of towels, I wish I had one. My skirt is disintegrating. It's the salt and the sun. I can see my orange underwear. If I were wearing pants with a crotch this wouldn't be a problem. Why do I even own orange underwear? Why do they even manufacture it? And who came up with the word "crotch"?

But it's not just my skirt that's coming undone. The exposure is wrecking my skin too. It's messing up all of our skin. Even if we do survive, I'm convinced that we'll all develop skin cancer. How can a person possibly absorb this much sunlight and be okay? My skin feels like it's baking. Around all the sores, I'm browning like a Thanksgiving Day turkey. It's awful, but not as bad as my thirst. I'd give my right foot for a drink of water. I'm surrounded by water, but I can't drink it. It's the sea. It's poison. My throat and lips are so dry that I've quit trying to form words.

Several times I've dreamed about walking into a green grassy field where I'm greeted by Rich Nixon. He wags his finger at me and surveys me with a disapproving face.

Rich Nixon: You said you were headed home.

Me: But if I had, I wouldn't have saved Burr.

Rich Nixon: Burr is gone. You didn't save anyone.

Me: Don't be an asshole!

I can hear my own hoarse, raspy voice. Sometimes the imaginary and real worlds blend.

"Enid, what's wrong? Who are you talking to? Who's the asshole? Nobody's doing anything," Wick says.

"Dude, relax," Dale says.

I don't need Wick worrying about me. That's not his job anymore.

"Whose turn is it to look for ships?" I ask.

"I'm looking," Sov says.

"Me too," Landon says.

"Good," I say. "I'm going to sleep."

"Enid!" Landon says. "I'm going to wake you up in an hour. I don't think it's good to stay asleep too long."

"Whatever," I say. All I want is to go somewhere else, somewhere there isn't this constant pain.

When I open my eyes, I'm looking at Nixon. Not Rich Nixon, but President Nixon. He's dressed in colorful Bermuda shorts, a white T-shirt, and is holding a cocker spaniel in the bend of his arm. He's got thinning gray hair and resembles very much the black-and-white rectangular photograph in my American History book. He's even got those fat, hamlike hands. I remember them from his official portrait, because I personally never know what to do with my hands when somebody takes my picture. Nixon is much taller than I realized, and he looks deadly serious. Wearing a pair of scuffed brown sandals, President Nixon hovers over the water next to me like a hologram.

"I'm Richard Milhous Nixon, the thirty-seventh president of the United States. This is my dog, Checkers."

"Oh God," I say. "I thought when you died you're greeted by a relative. I expected to see my Grandma Calhoun."

He laughs and sets the dog down in the water. But Checkers doesn't sink; he curls up at Nixon's feet.

"Well, I'm dead and you're not," he says.

"Why are you here?" I ask.

"Encouragement. I know what it's like to be down."

I don't say anything to him. In American History we've

recently read all about Watergate and Nixon's impeach-ment. But worse than that, we studied about his campaign, code-named *Menu*, to secretly bomb Cambodia. Lots of innocent people died.

"I know that you're judging me," he says. "I've been judged before. I can assure you, after you get here, you'll pay for all the wrongs you committed in your lifetime three times over."

"So you're telling me to repent?" I ask.

"Worse," he says. "I'm telling you to forgive."

"You mean my father?" I ask.

"We all make mistakes," he says.

"I can't," I say.

"The world needs more forgiveness," he says.

"I really can't," I say.

"You'll grow a crooked, wounded heart." He frowns at me. Checkers sniffs at the raft and lifts his back leg to relieve himself. He does it very near Dale's head.

"Am I going to live or die?" I ask.

"What do you want?" he asks.

"I want to live," I say.

"Well, then, make it an honorable life." He bends down and scoops Checkers back up, tucking him under his arm.

Checkers happily wags his tail. He squirms to get out of Nixon's grasp. "Thank you," I say. *Why am I thanking him?*

"Do you mind if he licks your face?" he asks. "It's something he likes to do."

I shake my head no. Checkers leaps into the raft and licks my cheeks and chin like we're long lost friends. It's painless. I guess ghost dogs don't have real flesh tongues. When he's done, Checkers flips around and jumps back into Nixon's arms.

"He's friendly," I say.

"He was an excellent dog in life, and he's proven to be a wonderful companion in death as well."

He looks at me and tightens his lips.

"Remember what I said about living an honorable life. It matters. Everything you say and do matters. Trust me."

"Not to be rude, but you look like you've done okay for yourself, and you weren't exactly the most honorable guy in the galaxy."

His lips loosen. He looks into the water.

"You have no idea where I'm headed. And no understanding of where I've been." He looks back at me. "And I didn't come here to tell you to forgive your father. I came here to tell you to forgive yourself."

And then, without any further elaboration about where he's headed, or where he's come from, or when or how I'm supposed to forgive myself, Richard Milhous Nixon and his little dog, Checkers, are gone, and it's just the blank sea stretching out into more blank sea again. I think of my parents. I look at Landon. I realize that I need to tell him what I did. I need to tell him that I called Grace. Even though he's going to be shocked and disappointed in me, I need to tell Landon all the awful things I said to her. My father isn't the only one who needs forgiveness.

chapter 23

It's no longer noon, but the sun is still up there, pounding us with its light. I look around the boat. Wick is asleep. He spent most of the night watching for a ship. Everyone else is wide awake, staring into the sea. I'm about to tell Landon about Grace, but Dale interrupts my plan.

"Dude, remember that game show where they stuck a bunch of people on an island?"

"You mean *Survivor*?" Landon asks.

"Yeah," Dale says. "Remember how they ate those rats, how they roasted them on sticks over a fire until they were pretty much charcoal?"

"Yeah," Landon says. "I remember that."

"I remember thinking they were a bunch of sick shits. But I'd eat a rat. I'm being serious. I really would."

I consider mentioning our earlier which-countries-eat-dogs debate, but decide it's best not to bring it back up. I swat at my ear. I keep hearing the sound of a mosquito.

Dale continues to talk, but not to anybody in particular. "My head is pounding. Is your head pounding? I look like a leper. I'm so hungry. And what are you swatting at?"

Has Dale been talking to me this whole time? It's hard to concentrate.

"I think it's a mosquito," I say. "But I also think it's just my imagination."

"Look!" Munny yells. "Fish! Fish!"

Because I'm pretty much a fatalist now, I expect to look over the raft's side and see a frenzy of hungry sharks. But when I peer over, that's not what's there. The water is darkened by a cluster of small, silvery fish. They're churning on top of one another. When they're out of the water, their bodies appear bluish black. They arch against one another, frenetically flipping their deeply forked tails. Dozens and dozens of heads pop out of the water, and some of their mouths appear to have something stuck to their lower jaws. I think they're worms. There's so many thrashing fish that they look like one solid thing, like a floating organism of fish. My mind starts working again.

"What are they?" I ask. "Can we eat them?"

"It's a shoal of menhaden," Munny says. "People don't eat them."

"Are they poisonous?" I ask.

"They're bony," Munny says.

Our raft has passed into the center of the large group of menhaden. I think if I just reached in the water, I'd be able to pick one up.

"Are you sure these are menhaden?" I ask.

"I've fished with my dad," Munny says. "We've used them as bait when we're trying to catch rockfish."

"If we can catch them, we can eat them," Sov says. "I don't care about their bones."

Sov and Munny are the first to thrust their hands in

the fish-packed water. Landon and Dale follow. I watch the menhaden scatter out of their fingers. They are so quick. And smart. They know we want to kill them. I'm so slow. I throw my opened hands into the water. I feel them swimming across my palms, escaping out of my loose fists. Then, finally, I catch one. It's pure luck.

"I got one!" I say.

"Me too," Sov says.

"What's going on?" Wick asks.

He gently shakes his head from side to side, trying to fully wake himself.

"We've found menhaden," I say. He glances at my flopping fish.

Wick looks at me and his jaw drops. I'm surprised he's this surprised. He looks over the side of the boat and sees the massive amount of fish. Then he looks into the sky.

"Oh my God!" he yells, pointing his finger to the sky. "Omega Protein!"

"What are you talking about?" Dale asks.

"That noise. That faraway whirring sound. It's a spotter plane from Omega Protein. They're out looking for menhaden. We need to stay with this shoal."

Wick leans over the side and starts paddling us back toward the thickest part of the fish.

"Dig deep," he yells. "We have to stay with them."

I guess we decide that it's okay if we lose a limb to a shark, because, almost in unison, we all throw our arms into the water. It reminds me of when we tried to row to Burr. No. Stop thinking about Burr. *Row. Row. Stay with the fish*. We use our arms like paddles, trying to pull the boat against the ocean's current. We're so tired, but we try to stay with the fish. I think we realize this could be our only and last chance to be rescued.

"Who the hell is Omega Protein?" Landon asks.

"They're a company." Wick is swatting his arms into the ocean, gasping to breathe, let alone talk. "They look for the menhaden in the air, then they send in ships. Then they vacuum them out of the sea. It's a terrible way to fish. That's why I donated money to Greenpeace."

I remember. He told me that, and then we broke up. Then he decided to pursue Simone. Then our boat sank. Then people I loved died. *Row. Row.*

"Terrible way to fish," Wick repeats.

But I don't say anything. If Omega Protein wants to rescue me, I'm totally willing to overlook their fishing methods. But we're not making progress. The school of fish are thinning out; we're moving past them.

"The log is slowing us down!" Wick says. "Lose it!"

"We might need it," Dale says.

"If we stay with the fish, we could get rescued," Wick says.

"Lose the log!" I say.

Dale doesn't let go of it.

"Make him, Landon," I say. "Make him!"

Landon moves to where Dale is gripping the driftwood.

"Help us, man," Landon says.

Wick, Munny, Sov, and I continue to try to stay with the fish. They're almost all gone. But if we stay close . . .

if we stay in a certain range, maybe the plane will see us.

"But what if the raft deflates?" Dale says. "We'd need it."

"No," I hear Landon say. "We don't have a lot of time left. Either we make it now. Or we don't make it."

Why can't Dale let go of the stupid log?

He finally does it. Dale and Landon join us. The splashing intensifies. We're all clawing at the water, trying to stay with the fish. I don't think I hear the plane anymore. I don't see the fish. But we're still in range. We have to still be in range.

"Sharks!" Sov yells, pulling his arms back into the boat. We all follow his lead.

The fins are popping up left and right. I am so tired. I really didn't have the energy to try to row the boat with my arms for much longer. I sit and hug myself. My sores are stinging. My muscles ache. And it's hard for me to catch my breath.

"Go screw yourselves, you lousy menhaden!" Wick yells.

He looks at me and smiles, not out of happiness, but out of disbelief.

"I gave Greenpeace money. Those asshole fish," he says. "Filter feeders. Menhaden control algae growth in coastal waters." He cups his hands over his mouth and yells at them, "Assholes!" Then he shakes his head at me. "Why wouldn't they stay with us? They should be good fish. Phytoplankton consumers. Their numbers drop, algal blooms multiply. Inshore waters become dead zones. They could have been good fish. Why wouldn't they stay with us?"

He's acting like I don't hate him. Why is he acting like that? Did I forgive him? I don't remember doing that. I didn't. I still hate him. I bury my face in my own body.

"They're fish. Their brains are the size of peas," Dale says.

"If people can't eat them because they're so bony, why does Omega Protein want them?" Landon asks.

"Bones and oil. They make lipstick and cat food out of them," Wick says.

Hate is too strong a word. I lift my head. I like that Wick knows random things. Science things. It's part of why I liked him. The random. The science. He continues to watch the shoal grow smaller and smaller. The whirr of the plane is totally gone now, if it was really even there at all. Wick's face literally droops from disappointment. But he keeps talking about the fish.

"They're loaded with omega-3 fatty acids. Food supplements. Health-crazed shoppers." He holds onto the dinghy with both hands, looking into the water. It's like a scene from a movie where the guy has to leave his lover behind. "They're turned into fish meal. Used in poultry and livestock feed. Used in cooking oils and margarine in Europe. Selfish. So selfish. What terrible fish."

His voice has grown so soft that I think he might have lost it. It's hard for any of us to talk for too long. I feel something slap against my foot. I look into the gross bottom water. It's my menhaden. I forgot all about catching a fish. I pick up one fish and Sov picks up the other.

All the guys circle around me and Sov. I know I should offer to divvy it up, but I follow my instincts, which are to stick the fish in my mouth and gnaw on its head. But my teeth are so sore that I can't break through the fish's skin. I take it out of my mouth and hand it to Landon. He tries too, but it's too thick for us. This fish's skin doesn't look tough, but our mouths are so weak that we can't chew it. Landon passes it to Dale. He closes his mouth around it several times. He, too, isn't able to break the skin.

"You are an asshole!" Dale yells. He throws it back into the water.

"Wait!" I say. "Maybe we could eat its eyeballs."

Now we're down to one fish. Sov holds it tightly with both hands. He tries to adjust his grip, so that he can move his thumbs closer to the fish's eyes. But the fish slips out of his grasp and lands in the raft's disgusting water. The fish thrashes at our feet.

"Get it!" Dale yells.

We all drop to our knees, trying to catch the flopping, dying fish. Sov quickly recaptures it between his hands and lifts it out of the water. He sets his thumbnail next to its watery eye, preparing to apply enough pressure to pop it from its soft socket. But he pauses.

"There's only two eyeballs and six of us," he says.

Dale looks eager and confused.

"There's not enough eyes to divide," Landon says.

"We should let it live," I say. "We should throw it back over."

"No way," Dale says. "Let's eat its eyes."

Sov pitches it over quickly, and the fish arches its body before it swims off. It actually seems appreciative.

"What a terrible fish," Wick says.

"Dude, acts of humanitarianism will only get us killed. From now on, we eat their eyes."

I don't know if Dale's right. I don't know if it will matter. These are the only catchable fish we've come across. I curl up into a ball. The bad water in the raft ebbs and flows across my deteriorating skin. This is so awful. This is worse than I ever imagined it could get. We could have been saved. There were planes in the sky looking into the water, and we were almost in their sights. I will never look at the sky again.

"Enid?" Landon says.

The way he says my name almost makes we want to tell him about Grace. I can feel Landon lightly tracing my initials on my leg. I don't tell him that I called her, because I'm not ready to admit to somebody that I called a fourth-grader and said the things I said. I know it was wrong. I shouldn't have blamed Grace. She's innocent. She didn't ask to be born. But at the time, I was so mad that I couldn't stop myself. Sometimes I'm like that. I let my emotions take over. Actually, I think that's why I'm in this lousy raft. My emotions. I let them control me. I need to use my head more. I have a brain. I need to use it. If we get saved, if I get to live, if God gives me that chance, I'm going to start using my brain all the time. I promise.

chapter 24

Sov and Munny are arguing over whether it's three or four o'clock. I don't care. It's not like I have to be anywhere. "Enid," Landon yells. "Enid, wake up."

"A ship?" I mumble.

"No, I just think you should stay awake for a while," he says.

I open my eyes. Sov and Munny no longer look identical. Munny has a shiner and Sov looks perfectly gray. In addition to being blessed with dramatically straight teeth, I think Munny also is predisposed to be tougher. His eyes don't appear as sunken. His body looks less lean.

"Enid, do you want to sit by me?" Wick asks.

I shake my head. Is he serious? No, I think. No. No. No.

"I'm so sorry about this." Wick practically groans his apology.

I hear myself say the word "Okay." I'm staring right at him. My head throbs and my legs feel wobbly.

"You forgive me?" he asks. Even though his eyes are sunken and yellowed, they look so happy.

I turn away. It's too soon.

"You said 'Okay,'" Wick says. "You forgive me?"

Why did I say "Okay"?

I think Wick is about to say something else, but Landon cuts him off. "Sort it out later."

I nod. I feel Wick's gaze leave me. I glance around the raft. I need to keep my mind working. I need to keep thinking. Not about Wick. About life. I need to rally.

It's hard to rally when I look at everyone. I can't believe how quickly we've all lost weight. Wick's face looks skeletal. I mean, I can see the outline of his bones beneath his skin. His eyes look like they've retracted back into his head. His cheekbones are protruding, and he's growing a beard. I never realized he had the potential to sprout this much facial hair. I close my eyes, intending to blink, but it's easier to just keep them closed. Half the time, when I shut my eyes, I hear a faint buzzing sound. I always pop them right back open and scout the skies for a plane. It happens again.

"What are you looking for?" Landon asks.

"A plane," I say. "Look, there, isn't that a plane?"

"It is," Landon says. "But it's an airliner. It's cruising at over thirty thousand feet. It'll never see us."

"Never?" I ask.

"I've seen about dozen of them," Wick says. "They're just too high."

I'm surprised that people have been noticing planes and not saying anything. It seems polite to at least point them out.

"Why are we so hung up on boats saving us?" I ask. "Couldn't a low-flying plane see us? Munny, has a plane ever spotted someone and rescued them at sea?"

Munny looks so tired. The bruise below his eye is bright purple. He weakly nods his head. "It has," he says.

I feel a new sense of hope. "How did it happen?" I ask. "Maybe we need to have somebody on plane watch."

Munny slowly shakes his head from side to side. "It doesn't matter if you spot the plane. The plane needs to spot you."

"How come you didn't tell us this sea rescue story when you told us about the others?" I ask.

"Because Landon said no more stories with torpedoes," he says.

"There's torpedoes in the plane rescue story?" I ask.

"Yes," he says. "Several."

"Tell us anyway," Landon says. "It'll give us something to do."

I rest my head against Landon's shoulder and feel myself relax into him.

"During World War II, an American cruiser, the USS *Indianapolis*, was struck by two torpedoes. The ship went down fast. About three hundred people were killed instantly, and another nine hundred went into the Pacific," Munny says.

"And then a plane came and got them?" I asked.

"Not at first. There was some sort of misunderstanding. Nobody came. They drifted in the water, injured, covered in oil. Some of the men were lucky enough to be in rafts."

"How long did they drift?" Landon asks.

"Four nights and five days," Munny says.

"We've been drifting almost that long," Dale says.

"Go on," I say. I want to hear how they were rescued.

"It was bad. There were a lot of burn victims. Some of them drowned. Some of them were eaten by sharks. Actually, a lot of them were eaten by sharks. Some just gave up. Finally, a plane flew over and saw them."

"Was it a friendly plane?" Dale asks.

"Yeah, it was an American bomber, and the pilot just came across them. It was a total coincidence. He saw the guys in the water and he wagged his wings, letting them know he saw them. But they were in the middle of the Pacific. It took time for people to get there. So the plane circled to keep them reassured, because by this point some of them were giving up."

"I can totally relate," I said. "How long before they were rescued?"

"Well, another plane showed up and saw a major shark attack, like thirty sharks taking sixty men, and so the pilot landed his plane in the water for them. And ships finally came. About three hundred men survived."

"I thought you said nine hundred went into the water," I say.

"Yeah, but there were a lot of sharks," Munny says.

"What kind of sharks?" Landon asks.

"Tiger sharks. Oceanic whitetips. Makos. Blue sharks. All sorts, I guess," Munny says.

"Dude, how do you know about this?" Dale asks.

"We read a book about it in Culture Club," Munny says.

"People think the ship had bad karma," Sov says.

"Why?" Wick asks. "What did it do?"

"The *Indianapolis* carried components of the atom bomb, Little Boy. That's the one that was dropped on Hiroshima. It killed eighty thousand instantly. And something like two hundred thousand people died later from the radiation."

"I thought there were two bombs," I say.

"Yeah, Little Boy was dropped first, by Colonel Tibbets, who flew the *Enola Gay*. Fat Man was the second bomb, dropped on Nagasaki. It killed about the same number of people."

"We never should have dropped those bombs on innocent people," I say.

Nobody says anything for a long time. That wasn't a very uplifting story. Too much death.

"Did the captain of the ship live?" I ask.

"He did," Munny says. "But he committed suicide twenty years later. Shot himself."

"Why?" I ask. "That's crazy. If you survived, why give up like that?" I'm shocked. I would never do that. None of us would ever do that.

"I'm not completely sure, but he used to get a lot of mail from parents who felt he was responsible for the accident. A lot of them blamed him for the deaths of their sons. Especially around the holidays."

"But it wasn't his fault," I say. "They were torpedoed."

"He was court-martialed for hazarding his ship by failing to zigzag. He was found guilty. I think that's why people blamed him."

"That's totally wrong," I say. "Somebody should do something to fix that."

"Somebody has. It's what this book *Left for Dead* was about. This middle-school kid did a report on it, because of something a character said in *Jaws*. Then a guy wrote a book about that kid's report," Munny says. "The kid met with a bunch of the survivors and the captain's family. They tried to get the captain exonerated."

"But he's dead," Wick says.

Ever since the menhaden got away, Wick has been a lot more depressed. I think about trying to cheer him up. But I'm not ready to talk to him. What would I say?

"All right," Landon says. "We need to switch topics. Listen, Munny, unless you've got something totally uplifting to say, you need to keep it zipped. We need hope. We need to focus on what's good in the world. No more Fat Man and Little Boy."

"I agree," Munny says. "I was just trying to answer Enid's question."

"Wait," I say. "What did the character in *Jaws* say that got this kid so interested in a World War II sea disaster?"

"Quint, the main shark hunter, talks about being in the water with the sharks after the ship went down."

"Doesn't that character get eaten by the shark?" I ask. Munny nods.

"That's so sad," I say, putting my face in my hands.

"I'm going to tell you what I hate about that movie," Dale says.

"You watched the whole thing?" I ask.

"I watched the whole thing," Dale says. "And it was a stupid movie. The entire film is a total moral lesson. I mean, who gets killed? All the people misbehaving. The naked chick on the beach who's messing around with that guy. Then, a bunch of horny teens who didn't listen to their parents end up biting it. It's like a Sunday school lesson with sharks. I never bought any of it."

"I guess," Munny says.

"You're wrong. Don't some of the good people die? Like the helicopter pilot or that poor dog?" I ask.

"It was a book before it was a movie," Munny said. "And the helicopter pilot gets killed in *Jaws Two*."

"Dude, what do you do? Sit around all day and watch *Jaws One* to *Four*?" Dale asks.

"Yes, Dale. I'm addicted to movies depicting unrealistic shark carnage."

"Shit!"

Water sprays over the raft as a lone motivated shark rams against the side.

"Shut up about *Jaws*," Landon says. "Fiction, nonfiction, half-fiction, we never need to mention that fish ever again."

None of us say anything else, which I guess is a form of agreement.

"Why is Sov so quiet?" I ask.

"Is he sleeping?" Landon asks.

"Sov. Sov," Munny says, shaking his shoulders.

Sov doesn't open his eyes.

"Hit him!" I yell.

"Calm down, Enid," Landon says. "Don't hit him, but shake him harder."

Munny hooks his hands on the life jacket and jerks Sov forward and backward several times. His head flops loosely. I'm scared he might not wake up. Then, suddenly, Sov's eyes blink open and he looks surprised.

"Is there a plane?" he asks. "I dreamed there was a plane."

The afternoon is setting in. The sun is lowering itself into the sea. We all look hopefully into the empty sky.

"No, we didn't see a plane," Landon says. "We just missed your company."

"Do I look that bad?" Sov asks. "That when I sleep I look dead?" Out of either fear or sadness, his dry lips tremble.

"We all look bad," Landon says.

"Let's bunk up," Munny says. He unfastens the straps on the life vest, and Sov pulls one of his arms out of an armhole. Munny inserts his own arm, and they squish together. Then, they rebuckle the straps. It's a tight squeeze, but they fit.

Dale looks at them and laughs.

"It's not funny," I say. We shouldn't laugh at each other. Even though, I guess it does look a little funny.

"I'm not laughing because of them," he says.

"Then why?" I ask.

He laughs harder. What's wrong with Dale? Is he going crazy?

"We're survivors," Dale says, sort of singing the words.

"I'm a survivor. You're a survivor. We're all survivors. We will not give up. We will keep drifting. Till we get home." He stops singing out loud but keeps moving his lips and rocking his head back and forth to some imagined beat.

It reminds me of a pop song, but I can't quite place it. Landon joins in every time Dale repeats "We're all survivors." And Sov and Munny add their voices to "We will keep drifting. Till we get home."

I stay silent, but Wick finally joins them. I can't quite manage the energy to sing. I can only listen and appreciate.

"I'm a survivor. You're a survivor. We're all survivors. We will not give up. We will keep drifting. Till we get home."

They repeat it several times. They sound defiant. It's as if our raft has manufactured a theme song. When they're finally finished, the mood feels lighter, but it quickly starts to fall.

"Enid," Wick says. "I want to sit by you."

I want to say no. But also want to say yes.

Wick moves to my side. I don't object. Do I want to stay mad forever? Forever. No. No. I'm a survivor. I shouldn't waste energy hating Wick.

I rest my head on Wick's shoulder and drift toward sleep. I don't want to be awake anymore. Sleep is easy. Sleep is better. Sleep feels good.

If I die at sixteen, I won't grow up. No going to college. No getting married. No becoming a vascular surgeon or a mother. I'm still a virgin. Dying now would be an enormous disappointment. I press my face against the side of the raft and gently bite at it. I know I can't eat it, but it gives me something to do. I have this feeling that if I allow myself to become motionless, I'll die.

There is a hand on my leg. It's Wick. Have I forgiven him? Not with words. But I don't hate him. I don't want him to die. Maybe there will be something else between us after this. After this?

I wonder if there is life after death. Would I go to college? Get married? Become a mother? I doubt it. I've never heard a word about sex in the afterlife. Maybe I'll get reincarnated. Do you get to choose what your soul inhabits? Could I come back as a goat? Or worse, some sort of edible vegetation? I don't think I want to be so stuck on death. My mind leaps. Machu Picchu. Wristwatches. My mother. A horse. Cake. Skate. My father. Grace. Burr.

I stare at my hand, entwined with Wick's. I move my fingers one at a time. I can't move my injured thumb at all. I can't believe a piece of glass can do this. Even when I touch it with my other fingers, I can't feel my thumb.

"Who do you think will get the money?" Dale asks.

"What money?" Landon asks.

"Skate and Burr's money. Who do you think will get it now? When their parents died, they got over a million bucks."

How can Dale be thinking about this? Why does it matter? Besides, the answer seems obvious.

"It'll go to his relatives," I say.

"Except for their uncle, they don't have any relatives. They're all gone," Dale says.

"Right," I say. It seems impossible, but the entire Riggs family has been extinguished in less than a year.

"So his uncle Bennett will get it," Munny says.

"That sucks," Dale says. "I didn't like that guy. Not looking out for them at all. I don't want him to get anything."

"Don't worry about that now," Wick says.

"So you met him?" I ask. I'm still trying to piece together the events.

"Briefly," Landon says.

"He was headed to Miami," Sov says.

"What a dick!" Dale says. "He should have stayed with them. That's what a good uncle would have done. And why did he even leave the keys for the boat?" Dale says. "He should have known they'd want to take it out."

"Maybe he didn't know," Sov says.

"None of this makes sense," Dale says. He sounds frustrated as he strings his sentences together. "It's like Burr and Skate had a death wish. We're out drinking on the night of a huge storm on a boat, and only two us know anything about sailing. Son of a bitch. Rewrite. Do over. We did it wrong. And Uncle Bennett becomes rich. Maybe he set it all up."

"No," Wick says. "It's a freak accident."

"I don't know," Dale says. "That guy shouldn't get anything."

"Stop," I say quietly. "Something else. I need to hear something else."

There is silence. I can hear myself moan. Landon moves toward me. "Enid?"

The raft feels unstable.

"Switch spaces with me," he tells Wick.

Wick agrees and moves to Landon's spot. We're not being as careful about weight distribution as we used to be. I guess we think it matters less and less.

"Landon?" I say.

I turn to face him, and I lace my fingers together like I'm going to pray. I can't keep my secret any longer. Landon has lowered his head right to my mouth. It's almost as if he can tell I'm going to make a confession.

"Tell me," he says.

"I called Grace."

He puts his hand on my knee. Landon has met Grace. Six months ago, he had an ice-cream sundae with her and my father at a Friendly's restaurant. I had refused to go. First, I'm not really a huge fan of Friendly's. Second, I didn't want to meet the product of my father's first affair. My father had another meeting scheduled with the two of us. Next week, Grace and my father and I were going to eat bagel sandwiches for lunch at a shop near Lake Champlain. Afterward, we were going to buy expensive chocolates. My father had told me that I had to go. But I would not, I'd told myself. I would not.

"When? What did you say?" Landon finally prompts.

"A week ago."

I don't say anything else. My head is pounding. Confessing doesn't make it feel any better.

"She's just a kid," Landon says. "It's not her fault."

I know he's right. But I don't know how to process it.

I nod. "I told her that I didn't want to meet her."

"What did she say?"

"She said, 'But you're my sister, Enid. I bet we'll like each other. I can count to fifty in Spanish.'"

I sniffle, but my nose is absolutely dry.

"What did you say?" Landon asks.

"I told her not to call me her sister. I told her I'd never like her. I said that my life would be better if she hadn't been born."

I search the cut on my hand. It's red and puffy and so swollen that it's breaking open. Landon doesn't say anything. I know he's ashamed of what I did. I feel his thumb on my chin. He presses on it, guiding my face to look at his.

"When we get out of here, you need to call her up and apologize. That was a shitty thing to do."

I nod. And I nod. And I nod.

"I feel awful."

"Enid, I know you're not ready to get past this yet, but one day you've got to get to a better place."

I bite my bottom lip.

"I know," I say.

"When we get out of here, you should probably talk to somebody."

He means a counselor. He takes hold of my chin again and makes me look in his eyes. His thumb feels weak.

"Okay," I say.

He closes his worried eyes. Beneath the thin skin of his eyelids, I think I can see his eyes darting from left to right. He must be in a place of dreams too. I wonder if President Nixon has come to him. Maybe he's like the patron saint of people adrift.

"Do you really think we'll get out of here?" I ask.

His eyes clap open.

"I do," he says.

His eyes aren't cloudy. They're clear. He seems certain.

"Do you think we'll all get out of here?" I ask.

He looks around the raft.

"I hope so," he whispers. "I hope so."

chapter 26

There's at least two hours of strong sunlight left. Then our fourth night will close in on us. We're talking less and less. It's as if the dinghy has grown rooms, and we've each taken our twin and found our own place to dwell.

We're so tired. I can hear it in the way we breathe. Frustrated sounds escape from our mouths when we exhale. Being this thirsty and worn down makes living laborious. None of us wants to talk. At the moment, it's easier not to. It's easier just to sit in one spot beneath the hot sun and be silent. And for me, this means that it's easier not to forgive.

I'm thinking about forgiveness. Not Grace. Wick. I haven't fully forgiven him. It's like I'm teetering on the lip of reversing course and unforgiving him altogether. I understand where President Nixon was coming from in his forgiveness lecture, but if your boyfriend lies to you, leading you to steal your mother's car and board a ship that eventually sinks, placing you on a dinghy adrift in shark-infested waters, I think it's okay to take some time to process the events. It could take me a few more weeks. Maybe months. Actually, I might be a retired grandmother living in Lancaster, Pennsylvania, trying to adjust to my newly replaced hip by the time I totally get over this.

It hurts. I don't hate Wick. I think I understand what happened. He was confused. We broke up. He got more confused. Enter Simone. And the end of my life. I get mad all over thinking about this. I haven't been this mad since those sharks nearly flipped our raft on day two. Actually, they've been trying to tip our raft relentlessly. I don't know why I'm stuck on the events of day two. I had no idea sharks were such focused fish. They have the determination of Olympians. I hate them. I listen to my breathing, then to the water. Its rhythmic splash begins to sound like the national anthem. I think back to the most recent Olympics. The Winter Games. I like watching figure skating and bobsledding. I don't really skate or sled. Skating hurts my ankles. I've never tried to bobsled.

Who among us would be the best at it? Maybe I would be. When I get back to my life, I should try it. I like that phrase: when I get back to my life. It runs through my mind on a loop.

"I'm going to try bobsledding." I hear myself say it out loud. "When I get back to my life."

"Really?" Landon asks. He sounds so groggy.

Now I remember that Landon is next to me. I like talking to Landon. I ask another question. "Besides humans, what animal do you think would be good at bobsledding?"

He doesn't answer. I look at him. He's fallen asleep. I poke him with my elbow and repeat my question. He pauses. I think he thinks I'm crazy. But then he answers me. I close my eyes.

"Penguins. They slide real well on their bellies. And

they can use their flippers to steer."

"You're right," I say. "They'd be great. Better than me."

I open my eyes and look into the ocean. Suddenly, in the white curling foam of the cresting waves, I think I see penguins. They're not bobsledding. They're walking upright across the water. Their clawed feet anchor their tuxedoed bodies as they waddle across the small waves. They have impeccable posture. They plod along with a sense of urgency. They act as if they've got somewhere they need to be. All of them.

"Look in the water. Do you see them?"

"What? Penguins?" he asks.

"Oh God, you do see them. They're really there?" My mind spins with worry. How far have we drifted?

"No, but I just mentioned them. It seemed like a likely hallucination."

"They're gone," I say.

"I've been seeing things too. Classic cars. They drive on the water like boats. They veer so close. Sometimes I feel like I could open up a door and climb inside."

"They're not real," I say. "Don't leave the raft."

"I know," he says.

Our mouths are spitless. Talking is tough. And my mind feels dull. I keep searching to find the right words. I'm amazed that I'm still able to stumble upon them. But I can. Landon and I are leaning into each other. We're nearly collapsed on top of each other, forming one person. Sov and Munny are similarly positioned. So are Wick and Dale. It's almost as if we're Siamese twins, attached to our respective twins somewhere around our hip regions. Also, I've experienced an emotional shift. Maybe it's related to the fact that we're approaching our last survivable day, but I've entered a new psychological space; it's a place of apathy. I don't know who or what to care about. There's one last question I want to ask. So I do.

"After you got back, would you have told me about Simone?"

"I don't know," Landon says.

"Oh, you would have, right?"

"Maybe, but it would've taken me a while. I might have just planted seeds of doubt. Dropped hints. Stuff like that."

It's almost like we're alone on the raft. I don't care if Wick hears me.

"Hey, I didn't know you read Noah's ark."

"What?" he asks.

"Day two. When you were chiming in about Noah's ark."

"I thought that was day one," he says.

"Maybe it was day one," I say. "You've read the Bible?"

"No, when I dated Lorna, sometimes I went to church with her. One Sunday there was a sermon on Noah's faith."

"You've been to church? What religion was she? Baptist?"

"No. Lutheran," he says.

Lorna had been Landon's first serious girlfriend. I had no idea she was religious. The only thing that stood out about her was that she had very big lips.

"Will you two get back together?" I ask. After dating for two years, they broke up right after Valentine's Day. He really hadn't started dating other girls yet.

"No, it's over," he says.

"Is it because she wants to date another Lutheran?" I ask.

"No. She ended up dating Skate for a while," he says.

"I forgot about that."

I think of Skate, not drifting away facedown in the ocean, but fully alive, jumping off the diving board into the pool, his knees hugged to his body, yelling, "Cannonball!"

"I don't want to think about Skate," Landon says.

I don't say anything right away.

"Did you love Lorna?" I ask.

"I don't want to talk about her," he says. "It's over."

"I was just surprised that you went to church with her," I say.

"It was only a few times," he says. "I went for her. Not for the sermons."

"I was surprised to hear you talking about the ark."

"Why? We went to Bible classes with Grandma Calhoun and learned about it. You had a needlepoint picture of it up in your room until you remodeled it last year."

"Oh yeah."

And suddenly, it's as if the picture is right in front of me. My grandmother, the only religious person in my life, passed away nearly a month after she finished it. The animals are gathered around the ark in twos. Their gender is distinguished by either the absence or presence of long, curling eyelashes. A pair of alligators kiss in front of the ark, while orange-beaked chickens perch on their backs. For the first time, I can see the humor in that—prey nestled atop predator. But my favorite part of the picture is the two happy giraffes, poking their heads out of two small windows. They crane their heads to look at each other. Their necks are long. It's clear that my grandma wanted me to know that they loved each other.

And behind the ark, and the united animal couples, there is the smiling sun. Literally: it has a smile line that connects the two apples of its exaggerated pink cheeks. It's nestled in a patch of blue clouds. But as I think about it now, I can't figure out whether the ark in the needlepoint is preparing for the flood or has already returned. Are the elephants stomping their way up the loading ramp, or parading their way back down? They're happy; the elephant in the rear position has its trunk entwined in the front elephant's small tail. But are they coming or going? Are they getting ready to abandon land, or are they rediscovering it? It seems so important. I can't believe that I never wondered about it until now. And where's Noah?

Something about approaching death allows a person to live in total clarity with whatever she can conjure in her head. That's where I am. Living in my head with this almost-forgotten picture. I watch it and then I let it fade. I still have a body. I can't completely retreat into my head just yet. It wouldn't be fair to the rest of me. I rub my neck against Landon's side. I never imagined dying this way. Until now, I'd contemplated two scenarios. A car accident. Or breaking one of the many thermometers in my house and releasing a stream of poisonous mercury, then somehow ingesting it. But never sharks. Never the open sea. Landon holds my good hand. He squeezes and I squeeze back.

"Enid, if I tell you something, will you promise not to think I'm a jerk?"

"Okay," I say. I have no idea where this confession is headed. I suspect it has something to do with a series of leg amputations that befell my Barbie collection in second grade.

"I can feel your pain," he says.

This seems like a very obvious comment.

"I know," I say. "We're all hurting."

"No, when the test administrators poke your toes, I can feel it. When they make you watch sad movies and you start to bawl, I can tell you're crying."

"What are you talking about?" I ask. This doesn't make any sense. "You mean sometimes you weren't honest during the twin tests?"

"No," he says. "Worse. I was never honest. I didn't want to be that connected to you. I wanted to be my own person. So I lied. I could always tell when you were eating Bing cherries. I could tell when you put your left foot in cold water. And I could tell when you were driving down here that you were really upset about something too."

"You knew I was driving down here?"

"No, but I could sense you were real frustrated. I could tell something was really wrong."

I don't even try to look at him. I remove my hand from his grip and slap him on the head with it.

"That was very selfish of you," I say. "And psychologically speaking, it totally could have messed me up."

"It was wrong. I'm sorry."

"So how connected are we?" I ask.

"You always knew when I was looking at a circle. Every time. It was unreal."

"Are we as connected as Burr and Skate?" I ask

"I think so. I mean, I don't know now that they're gone. I don't know what heaven is like."

"Do you think they went to heaven? How does the afterlife even work? Mormons aren't supposed to drink," I say.

"If heaven keeps out beer drinkers, the line into Hell is going to be astronomically long."

He leans in and kisses my head.

"Where did you get this barrette?" he asks.

"Dad gave it to Mom," I say. "I found it in the glove box. I think it was a guilt gift over affair number three."

"He's not perfect."

"I can't be with a guy who cheats on me."

"You don't have to be."

Landon leans his head against me, and the steady pressure hurts my neck. I turn my head up to look at him. He's sleeping.

"Landon?" I say.

He doesn't wake.

"Landon?" I whisper.

And I join him in sleep.

I hear the sound of a storm. The waves begin to quicken and heave against the raft. I know it's the end. I can't believe that I hung on this long only to die in a second storm. I start thinking about my funeral. Who will come? What will my parents dress me in? Maybe they'll put me in last year's prom dress. It's an icy blue color and falls just below my knees. It would be a shame to wear that dress only once. Wait. If I die this way they'll never find my body.

"My God!" Wick yells.

I turn to look at him. His finger trembles. He points to the sky. I look up. It's a bird. It's a big metal bird with glass eyes. Is this what takes us all to heaven? Do we all get to go there at the same time? I thought death would take us one by one, but the bird looks big enough for everyone. How am I supposed to get on this thing? Does it beam me up? Do girls go first? Sometimes, I feel like I don't know anything.

chapter 27

Thwack. *Thwack. Thwack.* As the bird hovers over us, the sea churns. It's so loud. I can't even hear myself think. The metal, heaven-bound bird has propellers that rotate over its head and swat the air. It doesn't appear angelic at all. I hope heaven isn't a world filled with robots and machines. I was expecting rainbows, marshmallow clouds, and maybe some puppies. But I guess I'll just live with whatever it is.

"Coast Guard!" Munny yells.

"Dude, he's right!" Dale says.

I can't believe it. I don't believe it. Less than a minute ago, I was planning my own funeral. It's hard to switch gears so quickly, to believe that, suddenly, I'm not going to die.

"Enid, you go first," Wick yells.

He's jerking his thumb at the bird.

"Yeah, you get in the basket first," Landon hollers.

I watch as a metal basket is lowered by a rope.

"I love you, Enid," Landon yells. "What's wrong? Are you afraid of the helicopter?"

I look at him. He's thrilled. Everybody is thrilled. The basket continues to drop, and I feel very calm. I look at Sov and Munny. They're unbuckling the jacket so they can separate themselves.

"I love the Coast Guard!" Dale cries.

Yeah, I think, I love the Coast Guard too. But after three days at sea, I'm boneless. I fall to the floor. Rotten salt water sloshes into my mouth. I spit it out. Landon grabs my arm and pulls me up.

"Save your energy for the basket," he yells.

The basket is halfway to us.

"Who goes after Enid?" Dale asks.

"Sov," Landon says.

I think that Dale is on the verge of disagreeing, when for some reason, he tries to sit on the raft's edge. It's too soft to support his weight. The next thing I see are his hands reaching to grab hold of the air in front of him. His body slips into the water. Actually, he doesn't slip so much as he plunges with a big splash.

"Dale!" Wick cries.

Wick stands up and immediately tips over, falling into the boat's bottom. He's facedown. I think he's passed out. Dale is bobbing helplessly in the Atlantic beside the dinghy. Several yards away from the raft, I see a gray fin lower itself beneath the choppy waves.

Sov and Munny hurry to Dale's side of the raft. They jump into the ocean. Some things are moving so quickly, while at the same time other things are happening in slow motion. The basket is arriving at a snail's pace. But the shark is approaching at lightning speed. I can see the top of its dark body as it swims toward Dale. Its head is shaped like a shovel. Maybe six out of eight was too high. Maybe we're going to lose one more. Maybe only five of us will survive. Or four. Or three.

Landon turns Wick over. If he doesn't, Wick'll drown. He rests Wick on his side and pats his back. Water flows out of Wick's mouth. He coughs. At the same time, Munny and Sov hook their arms around Dale and shove him onto the raft. I reach out and grab Dale, pulling him on board. He slides onto the floor of the raft, his muscles jittering beneath his skin. He didn't have enough strength to pull himself to safety.

Sov and Munny are still in the water. The shark is almost to them. It's approaching like a torpedo. They're not strong. They're the weakest among us. They jumped in without the life jacket. This is not fair, I think. *Help them. Help them.* I reach my arms out to them. Munny grabs onto the raft first. Sov flings his arms over a second later. It's unreal. They each grab one of my hands. I crouch and try to lower my center of gravity, anchoring myself. Landon sees what's happening and holds onto my waist. Sov's and Munny's shoulder muscles and biceps harden like stones as they both swing their bodies over the side, and roll on board. The shark lowers itself and swims underneath the raft. I look at them, stunned.

Wick continues coughing. Dale gasps for air. My mouth is open. Sov and Munny are breathing heavily, but they're not out of breath. Even with my help, they pulled themselves onto the raft without any problem at all.

"How did you do that?" I ask.

"Adrenaline," Sov says.

"Plus, we wasted as little energy as possible on that stupid log," Munny says.

It was a stupid log. It's like a villain. That's probably why Dale didn't have the strength to get back in the raft.

"Thank you," Dale says. His voice is desperately sincere.

"I couldn't let a shark get you," Sov says. "You're a survivor." He sings this a little, though it's hard to hear over the noise of the propeller.

"Oh my God. Oh my God," Dale says. He peels himself out of his sopping wet jacket and lets it fall to the raft's floor. He's touching his chest and legs and butt, checking himself. "It didn't bite me?"

"You're safe," Munny says. "Breathe."

"I don't think I need to try cocaine now," Dale says.

The basket is beside the dinghy. The wash of water created by the rotor is intense. I think it even scares away the shark. Landon pulls the basket to the raft and helps set me inside. It's like a stretcher with metal walls. I lean back and rest my head against a flotation buoy.

"You're saved," he says, kissing me on top of my head. I glance at Wick before I let go of Landon. Wick is still coughing.

I can barely hear the guys talk. They're figuring out who should go up next.

The basket is smoothly lifted by a machine in the helicopter. I watch the raft growing smaller. The guys look so puny down there. I can feel the basket reach the top. A man pulls me into the helicopter. It looks like he's wearing earmuffs and a wetsuit.

"Survivor at the cabin door," he says, setting me on the floor. "Survivor getting out of the basket."

I feel heavy and light at the same time. I can hear them talking. They're lowering the basket again. I stare out the door of the helicopter. I'm in the sky. Above the water. I'm alive. I wonder who I'll see next. Probably Sov. That makes sense. I feel somebody pull me farther away from the door.

"Welcome aboard. I'll get you some water. Then I'm going to give you an IV."

I've collapsed. I feel like I'm going to be unconscious soon. But I feel a sharp pain in my head. I'm leaning against a wall, and my barrette is digging into my scalp. Why did I even wear this thing? Why did I even keep it? Like hair really matters when you're adrift at sea. I reach to take it out. The man sees what I'm doing. He unclips it and presses it into my hand.

"You'll want to save that. That's how we found you. It reflected the sun and caught Daphne's eye." The man points to the pilot. She must be Daphne. I didn't realize Coast Guard pilots were women.

Holy shit, I think to myself. *This trinket saved me. This stupid trinket saved us all.*

Holding the barrette in my hand, I feel a pinch on my arm. It must be the IV. I'm so tired. I can hear the rope whistle as the basket rises again.

"You've been all over the news," a voice says. "Eight teens adrift. It's a national story."

I don't respond. I don't care about that. It's over. And

we're not eight. We're only six. But we're safe.

The basket arrives and it doesn't hold Sov. It's Wick. I lift myself off the floor a little. My heart quickens and I feel myself filling with excitement. He's pulled from the basket and he crawls toward me. He drapes an arm over me and the rest of his body collapses. We lie down beside each other. We don't say anything. For the first time since Wick walked out of my kitchen, what's happening feels like what should be happening.

"Enid," he says. His arm tries to pull my body closer to his.

"Wick," I say, as I let myself be pulled.

Thank God. Thank God. This is what it feels like to be rescued. Wick and I don't say anything else. I wonder who is in the next basket.

"Survivor at the cabin door."

I am barely able to lift my head. It's Dale. Sov and Munny and Landon sent Dale next. I close my eyes. Sov will be next. Then Munny. Then Landon. We're all making it. We survived.

Thwack. Thwack. Thwack. The helicopter blades cut though the air so powerfully that they vibrate my bones. They create a spectacular rhythm inside of me. For some reason, suspended in midair, I think of the ark, and the animals galloping off the boat to feel their own weight on land again. I'm not thinking of the animals in the needlepoint, but real flesh-and-blood animals. Their hoofed and clawed feet pounding against the newly rediscovered muddy earth. Myth or not, I think I know how it must have felt to arrive after the flood.

As I drift to sleep beside Wick, I hear them thundering over the earth. *Thwack. Thwack. Thwack.* The sound sings through me and delivers me to a place of dreams, where there is land, and there is life, and there is joy.